# ONE NIGHT IN PARIS

**SANDI LYNN**

# ONE NIGHT IN PARIS

*New York Times, USA Today & Wall Street Journal*
*Bestselling Author*
Sandi Lynn

**One Night in Paris**

Copyright © 2019 Sandi Lynn Romance, LLC

All rights reserved. No part of this publication may be reproduced, distributed, or transmitted in any form or by any means, including photocopying, recording, or other electronic or mechanical methods without the prior written permission of the publisher.
This is a work of fiction. Names, characters, places and incidents are the products of the authors imagination or are used fictitiously. Any resemblance to actual events, locales, or persons, living or dead, is entirely coincidental.

Cover Photo by Wander Aguiar
www.wanderaguiar.com
Models: Florian & Laura
www.wanderbookclub.com

Cover Design by Shanoff Designs

Editing by BZ Hercules

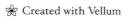 Created with Vellum

## MISSION STATEMENT

**Sandi Lynn Romance**

*Providing readers with romance novels that will whisk them away to another world and from the daily grind of life – one book at a time.*

# CHAPTER ONE

*Anna* Each of my bridesmaids gave me a hug and left the bridal room to go take their places. A few moments after they left, there was a light knock on the door, and when I opened it, my best friend, Franco, stood there holding my veil.

"Your veil." He grinned as he stared at me from head to toe. "You look absolutely beautiful, Anna."

"Thank you. Get in here!" I smiled as I pulled him inside the room.

I stood in front of the three-way mirror and stared at my reflection.

"You really outdid yourself with my wedding dress," I spoke to him.

"You deserve only the best, Anna." He smiled as he placed the veil he made on my head. "Are you okay?"

"Yeah. I'm fine."

I walked to the balcony and stared out at my future husband waiting for me with approximately two hundred guests who had properly taken their seats.

Franco took hold of my hand and lightly gripped it as he stood next to me.

"You don't have to do this. There is always plan B."

"I know. I better get down there. I'm late and my dad's going to kill me."

He let go of my hand, held out his arm, and walked me to the back of the hotel and down the stairs, where my father waited for me.

"You're late," my father spoke as I took hold of his arm. "That is disrespectful to Matthew and your guests, Anna."

"Franco had to fix a button on my dress. It came loose."

The music started to play, and I took in a deep breath. My stomach was tied in knot after knot walking down the white runner as every single guest stared at me. This was what was expected of me. But the thing was, I was never good at doing the expected. I stared at my future husband as he stared back at me. Even his stare was annoying. We were almost to the end of the aisle when I came to an abrupt stop. It was now or never. I chose now.

"I'm sorry, Dad," I spoke as I turned to him and placed my hand on his cheek.

"Anna?"

I turned around, kicked off my heels, and ran up the aisle, throwing my wedding bouquet behind me with a smile on my face. I heard both my father and Matthew shouting my name, but I ignored them and kept running. I ran up the steps, into the hotel, through the lobby, and out the front door, climbing into the black limo that was parked along the curb.

"So you did it." Terrance, my driver smiled.

"I did it. Thanks for waiting for me."

"Not a problem, Anna. Airport?"

"Yes." I smiled.

Freedom and exhilaration soared through me as the plane took off from LAX. I was on a high. Something I always got when I was defiant. I was a strong-willed, independent woman and when someone told me to do something, I always did the opposite. I'm not going to lie, Matthew wasn't the love of my life. Why did I accept his marriage proposal? Because it was what my father wanted. I thought for once I'd grown up and I could make him proud. He brought Matthew into the company to groom him and to run it with me one day. That was how we met. He was practically shoved down my throat every single day and he was persistent about taking me out. So I finally gave in and went on a date with him. He was good-looking, and the rest is history. He grew on me, but I wasn't happy at all. I just went with the flow, worked, and planned my wedding. The way he kissed my father's ass was annoying. In fact, everything he did was annoying. Even the sex with him was annoying. I faked more orgasms than I had real ones. I gave myself better orgasms than what he could give me.

The plane touched down in Paris, and as soon as I turned on my phone, there were numerous text messages and missed calls from my father, with the exception of one text message from Franco.

*"I knew you'd do it. Call me when you get to Paris, regardless of the time."*

I took a cab to the Peninsula, where reservations were made for Mr. & Mrs. Matthew Bondi. Yep. I did it. I took our honeymoon anyway. I loved Paris and I needed the escape.

"Bon jour." The man behind the desk smiled.

"Bon jour. Reservations for Bondi," I spoke.

"I'm sorry, Mrs. Bondi, but that reservation was cancelled yesterday."

I rolled my eyes. "Of course it was. And for the record, I never became Mrs. Bondi. I left my fiancé at the altar and I'm still Anna Young. So, since my honeymoon suite was cancelled, I'm going to need a room. The Garden Rooftop suite if available."

"I'm sorry, Miss Young, but that suite is booked. I can put you in our Katara Suite that's right next door."

"The Katara Suite will be fine." I smiled.

"Very good. I'll have someone bring up your bags."

I took the elevator up to the sixth floor, and as I was sliding my keycard to unlock the door, I noticed an incredibly sexy man walking out of the Rooftop Garden Suite next door.

"So you're the one who took my suite." I smirked as he passed by.

"Excuse me?" He stopped and turned around.

"Nothing. It was a joke. I just flew in and I wanted that suite and they told me that it was already booked."

"Well, we could always share it if you want it that badly." A sly smile crossed his perfectly handsome face.

"I'm sure your wife wouldn't appreciate it."

"I'm not married."

"Oh. Well, then your girlfriend wouldn't appreciate it."

"No girlfriend either. It's just me in there."

"I'm good with this suite but thank you for the offer." I blushed.

"If you change your mind, you know where to find me. I need to run. I'm late for a meeting." He smiled.

I sighed as I watched his six-foot-two stature and fine ass walk down the hallway in his tailored designer dark gray suit that fit him perfectly in all the right places. His brown hair was kept short all the way around with a slightly longer top, which had a wavy texture to it, and his rich brown eyes were captivating as they held me in a trance. In fact, every feature on his face was captivating. Damn, that man was sexy.

I opened the door to my suite and stepped inside with a smile on my face.

"Welcome to Paris, Anna," I spoke as I looked around.

## CHAPTER TWO

*Anna*

I threw myself on the king-size bed and called Franco.

"I've been waiting for you to call," he answered. "How's Paris?"

"Beautiful as always. How's my dad?"

"Shouldn't you be asking how your ex-fiancé is?"

"I'm sure he's heartbroken and I really don't care."

"Well, your dad is pissed as hell and your step monster mommy wasn't happy about it either. As for Matthew, he called you every name in the book. He said you humiliated him and that he won't take you back when you realize you made a mistake and come back crawling on your hands and knees begging for his forgiveness."

"Ha." I laughed. "I'm not going back. Speaking of which, are you at my apartment?"

"I am. I'm packing the rest of your clothes up now."

"Thank you. I'll call the movers tomorrow and have them put my furniture in storage and bring the rest of my things to New York. I just couldn't do it, Franco, and when I saw him standing there, everything became so clear."

"I know, but damn, you looked good running away in that dress. By the way, Terrance dropped off the dress."

"Good. I'm sorry you have to drag that all the way to New York."

"It's not a problem, my dear. I'll make sure I have everything ready for you when you get there."

"Thanks, Franco. I don't know what I'd do without you."

I ended the call and changed my clothes for dinner. As tired as I was, my belly wouldn't stop growling. I headed over to L'Oiseau Blanc up on the rooftop, and when I arrived, they were packed.

"Bonjour. May I help you?" a cute blonde hostess asked.

"I was hoping to get a table for dinner."

"Do you have a reservation?"

"No. I just flew in."

"I'm so sorry, but we are completely booked, and as you can see, we're full."

"She's with me." The handsome man from the hallway smiled.

"Oh look. I'm with him." I grinned at the hostess.

He held out his arm and led me to his table, where he graciously pulled a chair out for me.

"Thank you. How did you know I was over there?" I asked.

"I was on my way back from the restroom and I saw you. I also heard the hostess tell you the restaurant is full, so I took it upon myself to invite you to sit with me." He smiled.

"Wow. First you invite me to stay in your suite and now dinner. Either you're a one in a million gentleman or you're trying to get me into bed."

"I won't lie. My bed would be a lot warmer with you in it." He winked.

I gulped as my belly fluttered and an overwhelming sensation hit me down below. Shit. This man was intense.

"Wine?" he asked as he held up the bottle that was sitting on the table.

"Oh god no." I quickly grabbed the glass before he could pour it. "If you don't mind, I'd like a neat martini."

"Of course." He signaled for our waitress. "So what is a beautiful woman like yourself doing in Paris alone?"

"How do you know I'm alone?" I playfully smirked as the waitress delivered my martini.

"Well, you were entering your room alone, and you said YOU just flew in. All that led me to believe you're here alone."

I sighed as I took a sip of my drink.

"I am here alone, and before I get into the gory personal details of why, I really should know your name. I don't like airing my dirty laundry to total strangers."

"I'm Westin, but you can call me Wes." He extended his hand across the table.

"And I'm Anna. You can call me Anna. Not Ann or Annie. Just Anna." I placed my hand in his and felt a thousand volts of electricity run through me.

*Damn.*

"So, Anna, now that we're not strangers anymore, feel free to air your dirty laundry." A smirk crossed his lips.

"I'm on my honeymoon." I finished off my drink.

He sat across the table and studied me while he slowly narrowed his eye.

"You're on your honeymoon alone?"

"Yes. I'll have another neat martini." I held up my glass. "I'm a really bad person, Wes. In fact, you probably don't even want to associate with me. I got halfway down the aisle, took one look at him, turned around, ran as fast as I could, climbed into the limo that was parked outside the hotel, and had the driver take me to the airport."

"You're serious, aren't you?" His brow arched.

"I'm afraid so." I slowly nodded.

"Why?"

"It's a long and complicated story that I don't want to bore you with. So the shortened version is that my father wanted me to marry him and I just couldn't do it."

"I see. Were you not in love with the poor guy you left standing at the altar?"

"No. I wasn't, and I wasn't happy. Like I said, it's a long, boring, and complicated story. I really don't want to waste our dinner time talking about it. I'm a bad person and I'm sure karma will get me big time for what I did."

"Don't be hard on yourself, Anna. You had to do what was best for you. Have you spoken to him at all since you ran away?"

"No. But my father has been blowing up my phone and I haven't answered him yet."

"Don't you think you should? I'm sure he's worried sick about you."

"I will." I lightly smiled. "On my own time. This isn't new to him, so I can guarantee you that he's not worried. More pissed off is like it."

"Am I to assume you've done this sort of thing before?"

"Ditch a man at the altar?" I laughed. "No, but I'm a little on the defiant side. So, on to you. I'm assuming you're here on business since you're staying in this hotel by yourself?"

"I am. In fact, I catch a flight home tomorrow."

"And where's that? Wait." I put up my hand. "Don't tell me. I don't want to know. This will be a memory for me."

"And what memory is that?" The corners of his mouth curved upwards before taking a sip of his drink.

"Meeting a nice man I know nothing about in Paris who offered me to stay in his suite and have dinner with him when I couldn't get a table."

He let out a chuckle.

"Okay, then. Same goes for me. You are the nice woman I met who left her fiancé at the altar, flew to Paris alone for her honeymoon, and was kind enough to let me buy her dinner." He gave me a wink and I tightened my legs.

## CHAPTER THREE

### Wes

This woman was stunningly beautiful. Her brown hair was long and flowed in waves over her shoulders. You could see her bright blue eyes from across the room as well as her bright smile. The one thing I noticed earlier while I stood talking to her in the hallway was her five-foot-seven stature and lean body. A body that was beautifully clothed. I could only imagine what it truly looked like naked. My imagination ran wild as my cock started to rise. With any luck, maybe she'd come back to my room for the night. I could make her forget about what she had done to her ex-fiancé, at least for one night.

We made small talk about Paris. It was best we didn't know anything about each other. Why make things complicated? After we finished off a few drinks and our dinner, I paid the bill and escorted her out of the restaurant. We took the elevator up to the sixth floor and I walked her to her room.

"Thank you for dinner. That was sweet of you." She smiled as we stood outside her door.

"You're welcome. Thank you for keeping me company. How about one more drink before we call it a night? I have a bottle of champagne in my room that has yet to be opened." I smiled as I lightly took hold of her hand.

"I think one more drink would be nice. After all, I would hate to see a perfectly good bottle of champagne go to waste, especially since you're leaving tomorrow." Her finger lightly trailed down my chest.

A wide grin crossed my lips as I led her to my room and opened the door.

"I'm going to use the bathroom real quick," she spoke.

"Go ahead. I'll get the champagne."

I popped the cork and poured us each a glass with the hopes we'd be drinking it in the bedroom. Obviously, Anna, had the same thing on her mind, because when I looked up, she stood across the living room in just her bra and lace panties.

"I hope you don't mind." She smiled.

"No." I grinned. "I definitely don't mind. Not at all." I slowly walked towards her as my cock rapidly rose to the occasion.

Her body was a wonderland, just as I fantasized about. She was sexy as fuck and I couldn't wait to devour every inch of her. I wrapped my arm around her waist, pulled her into me, and softly brushed my lips against hers. There was no way in hell I was rushing this, no matter how badly my cock throbbed. We stood there, our lips locked together as our tongues intercepted and found their way to each other. I took my hand and softly ran it down her torso, feeling the softness of her skin and rock-hard abs as it made its way down the front of her panties. She was freshly shaven and already wet, which heightened my excitement. I dipped my finger inside her and she gasped as my tongue stroked the flesh of her neck.

As I explored her, her fingers fumbled with my belt and then my pants as she successfully took them down. I wasn't about to stop what I was doing until she came. I would make sure she had multiple orgasms tonight. Her hand wrapped around the shaft of my hard cock and I moaned while my lips traveled to her cleavage. I couldn't wait to see her tits out of that black lace bra she was wearing. The more I explored her, the more she moved her hand up and down me. She was skilled at giving a hand job and I was already about to come.

"Anna," I whispered. "You have to stop. I'm going to come."

She quickly released her hand and let out a loud moan as she came. I removed my finger and ran it up her torso as I undid her bra with my other hand. Fuck. She was perfect. I tossed her bra on the floor, stepped out of my pants, quickly tore off my shirt, and swooped her up and took her into the bedroom. I laid her on the bed, and after devouring her breasts, my mouth traveled down her wonderland of a body and to her pussy, which was dripping in wetness. I took it all in and explored every inch of her below the waist. She threw her head back in pleasure as delightful moans escaped her.

"Oh god," she repeated over and over again. "Yes. Holy shit, yes! Whatever you're doing down there, don't stop because I'm going to come again."

She grasped the comforter in her hands and howled while her body tightened, and I felt her warmth on my lips. I stood up and looked around.

"Shit. My pants are in the other room. Stay exactly how you are." I pointed at her.

"You don't have to worry about that. I can't move at the moment." She grinned.

I ran to the living area, grabbed my pants that were on the floor, and took out my wallet, removing a condom from it. Quickly tearing the corner with my teeth, I took it from the package and rolled it over my harder-than-ever cock. I walked back into the bedroom and hovered over Anna as I softly kissed her lips.

"Now, where were we?"

She wrapped her arms around my neck.

"I do believe you were going to fuck me." She grinned.

"Ah, that's right," I spoke as I thrust inside her.

We both let out a sound as I slowly pushed into her, inch by inch until I was buried deep inside. Our lips met again, locked in a passionate deep kiss as I continued to thrust in and out of her. Her nails dug into my back as I picked up the pace and soft moans escaped her lips. I halted and rolled on my back as I brought her on top of me. She rode me for a while, and damn, she was amazing. I brought her down to me, kissed her beautiful mouth, and rolled her on her back to finish the job. An orgasm tore through her as the sensation in my cock built stronger and stronger until I could no longer hold it. One swift thrust and I exploded.

I rolled onto my back and tried to catch my breath. Looking over at her, I saw she had a grin across her face. I smiled back, removed the condom, and tossed it in the trash can next to the bed.

"Stay here tonight," I spoke as I stroked her arm and she laid her head on my chest.

"I'm actually going to take you up on that offer because I'm too tired to even try to get out of this bed. What time do you need to leave tomorrow?"

"I need to leave the hotel around eleven a.m. So that'll give us time to have breakfast before I go."

"Sounds good. Good night, Wes."

"Good night, Anna."

## CHAPTER FOUR

*Anna*

I lay there with my head resting on his muscular chest as I listened to the soft beats of his heart. I had never in my life experienced sex the way I did with him. He was a master and a god, and my body was still in shock. Shit. I sat up and grabbed my phone.

"What are you doing? I thought you were sleeping," Wes spoke.

"I have to call my dad. Just be quiet, okay?" I smiled as I turned on the lamp.

"Sure." He laughed.

"Anna Renae Young!" he shouted as he answered. "What the hell is going on?"

"Dad, I'm sorry, and in case you're wondering, I'm fine."

"Well, I'm glad someone is. Do you realize what you've done?"

"Yes, I am fully aware of what I've done. I put my happiness before anyone else's."

"Even at twenty-seven years old, you manage to make my blood pressure rise. Aren't you even going to ask how Matthew is doing?"

"I was just getting to that. How is he?"

"He's pissed, humiliated, and hurt! That's how he is, and he doesn't want to talk to you."

"Okay. Then he doesn't have to talk to me. I didn't love him, Dad. I'm sorry to disappoint you, but it's my life. He didn't make me happy."

"No one will ever make you happy, Anna."

"Did you really want me to marry a man I wasn't in love with?" I asked in a stern voice.

"Matthew is a good man with a promising future, and you treat him like he's scum on the bottom of your shoe. You should be ashamed of yourself."

"The only thing I'm ashamed of is almost settling because I didn't want to disappoint you."

"Well, you ended up disappointing me again, Anna, and I'm afraid that I can't have unreliable people working at my company. Whenever you decide to come back, you won't have a job."

I swallowed hard, even though I was prepared for this.

"I'm sorry you feel that way, Dad. But look on the bright side. You lost a daughter and gained a son. I hope you and Matthew are happy together."

I pushed the end button on my phone and gently set it down.

"Anna," Wes softly spoke as he reached over and placed his hand on my back.

"Hey, it's all good. I was prepared for this." I took in a deep breath as I fought to hold back the tears.

"I'm sorry," he spoke.

I took in another deep breath and then let a smile cross my face as I leaned over and brought my face to his.

"I'm up for another round if you are?"

"Definitely." His lips met mine as his arms wrapped around me.

I awoke to someone knocking on the door. When I opened my eyes, I saw Wes wasn't next to me. Slipping on the hotel robe, I walked out into the living area, where breakfast had been delivered and set up.

"Good morning." Wes smiled. "I hope you're hungry."

"Good morning. I'm starving. What did you do, order the entire breakfast menu?" I asked as I stared at all the silver platters with lids over them.

"I didn't know what you liked. So I got us scrambled eggs, pancakes, French toast, eggs benedict, bagels, yogurt, fresh fruit, croissants, and coffee and tea," he said as he lifted each lid.

"Well, to be brutally honest, I like all of it. Let's dig in." I grinned as I sat down.

He took the seat to my left and we shared a scrumptious breakfast.

"How long are you staying in Paris?" he asked.

"I'll be here about a week." I smiled as I bit into my bagel.

"Are you going to be okay here by yourself?"

"Of course. Why? Do you want to stay and keep me company?" A smirk crossed my lips.

"Don't tempt me. I would love to, but I need to get back to the States. Work calls." He picked up his phone and looked at the time. "I really need to go get ready. I have to leave soon."

He got up from the table and I finished my breakfast. When I was done, I walked into the bedroom and grabbed my clothes and my purse.

"Thank you for dinner, breakfast, and the amazing sex." I smiled as I stuck out my hand to him.

He stood in front of me and placed his hand in mine. My heart started to rapidly beat.

"It was my pleasure, Anna," he spoke as he brought my hand up to his lips. "Good luck with everything. I hope whatever your next adventure is, it works out for you."

I gave him a heartfelt smile as I slowly removed my hand from his and began walking towards the door. I stopped for a moment and turned around.

"It was really nice to meet you, Wes."

"It was nice to meet you too, Anna."

I walked out of his room and over to mine. The moment I stepped inside, I felt like I'd been punched in the gut. I'd done the walk of shame plenty of times, but this one was different. I pulled my phone from my purse and facetimed Franco.

"Anna," he sleepily answered. "Everything okay?"

"I need to talk to you. It's important!"

He turned on his bedroom light and put on his black-rimmed glasses.

"Oh. Who's that?" I smiled as I caught a glimpse of a man lying next to him.

Franco got out of bed and went into the living room.

"That's Thaddeus. We met at the airport. Don't ask."

"Oh. So I guess we both did the walk of shame together."

"What are you talking about? Did you sleep with someone there already?"

"Franco, I have no words. He was the best sex I'd ever had. I had multiple orgasms. I didn't think it was possible, and he is so sexy."

"Way to go, Anna banana. Fucking a sexy Frenchman. You make me proud to call you my BFF."

"He's not French. He's American and he was here on business. Unfortunately, he's on his way to the airport now to go home."

"And where is home for this sexy American who gave you multiple orgasms?"

"I don't know. I told him not to tell me. I didn't want to know a thing about him. I'm storing this as a memory. One night in Paris with a sexy American that I met while I was supposed to be on my honeymoon."

"Did you at least get his name?"

"Wes."

"Wes what?" he asked.

"I didn't want to know that either. It happened, he's gone, and I'm going to enjoy the rest of my vacation alone. By the way, I talked to my dad. He fired me."

"What? Are you serious? He can't do that. You're his daughter."

"Good thing I moved my money, just in case."

"I don't know what to say. I'm sorry, but you're better off."

"I know I am." I gave him a soft smile. "Listen, go back to your boy toy and I'll see you in a week."

## CHAPTER FIVE

*Wes*

My trip was pretty boring until I met Anna. Figures we'd meet on my last night in Paris. At least we shared one night together. A night I wouldn't forget any time soon. She captivated me, and it had been a long time since any woman had done that. I'd slept with a lot of women. Women who only seemed to care about my money. Anna didn't seem that way, but then again, she didn't know who I really was. After I landed, I went home to my Park Avenue penthouse and set my suitcase on the bed. When I opened it, I found a pair of Anna's panties with a note pinned to them.

*"Just a small reminder of our one night together. Thank you. Sincerely, Anna."*

A smile crossed my lips as I held them up. My cock started to twitch, so I tucked them in my drawer as a reminder of her. Damn it. I should have stayed another day or two, but I couldn't. I needed to be back for an important meeting, one I couldn't afford to miss. Plus, why make things more difficult.

~

The next morning, as I approached my office, I could tell something was off with Chrissy, my personal assistant.

"Welcome back, Wes. I need to speak with you."

"Of course. Come into my office."

I walked in and set my briefcase down while Chrissy took a seat across from my desk.

"What's going on?"

"I don't know how to say this, so I'm just going to come right out with it. I'm giving you two weeks' notice."

"Why?" I asked with surprise as I cocked my head at her.

"Now that Tom and I are divorced, I decided to move back home to Seattle to be with my family. I really hate doing this to you, but I can't stay in the same state as him any longer."

"I understand." I folded my hands. "Do you have a job lined up there?"

"No." She looked down. "I'm going to look when I get there."

"You were a great personal assistant and it's going to be very hard to fill your shoes. I can make a few calls to my contacts in Seattle and see if I can get you a job." I smiled.

"Really?" She looked up at me.

"Yeah. Give me a day or two and I'll let you know."

"Thanks, Wes. Again, I'm sorry to do this to you."

"Don't worry about it. You have to take care of you. I understand why you have to leave." I gave her a small smile as I got up from behind my desk and walked over to her. "It's going to be very hard to replace you." I gave her a light hug.

I felt bad for her. She was a woman in her mid-forties and an attractive one at that. She had been married to her husband for twenty-one years before she found out about his mistress and the affair that had been going on for the past three years. I didn't blame her for wanting to move away, not one bit. I sighed as she walked out and shut the door. Picking up my phone, I called down to human resources to let them know and to find me a replacement for when she left.

"Welcome home, Wes." Christopher, my friend and vice president, grinned as he walked into my office.

"Thanks, Christopher."

"How was Paris?"

I stared at him with a wide grin splayed across my face.

"What?" His eye steadily narrowed at me.

"I had the best one-night stand of my life my last night there."

"Do tell." A sly smile crossed his lips.

"Her name is Anna and she is the most beautiful and sexy woman I've ever met. She was staying in the suite next to mine. We had dinner together and then spent the night in my room."

"Did you get her number?"

"Nah." I leaned back in my chair. "I'll never see her again. She was on her honeymoon." I smirked.

"Wait. What?" He lightly shook his head.

"She left her fiancé at the altar. Took one look at him walking down the aisle and then bolted and flew to Paris."

"Damn, Wes. Sounds to me like she has some problems."

"Maybe." I shrugged. "At least she knew what she didn't want. You have to give her credit for that. She called her father while we were together, and they had a huge blow-up. I couldn't quite hear what he was saying, but it was something about her disappointing him again."

"She sounds like a rebel to me," Christopher spoke.

"Perhaps. I have no idea where she's from or where she's going to go. But the one thing I can tell you is that I can't stop thinking about her. I haven't felt this way in a long time."

"It was probably best you left it the way you did. You didn't tell her who you were or what you did, did you?"

"No. She only knows me as Wes."

"Gotta love those one-night stands. Sometimes they can really leave a mark on us. Well, you had a night of great sex and fun. At least you don't have to worry about her using you for your money and status." He smirked.

He left my office as I turned my chair around and stared out into the busy streets of New York City and thought about the little gift she left me in my suitcase.

# CHAPTER SIX

*Anna*

I landed in New York City, and when I went to get my luggage, I saw Franco standing there waiting for me with a smile on his face.

"Bonjour, Madame." He held out his arms.

"It's so good to see you." I smiled as I hugged him.

"How was Paris besides fucking the sexy American?"

"It was nice. I did a lot of shopping." I grinned.

Franco grabbed my luggage and we headed to his car. When we arrived at his Tribeca apartment on West Broadway, he took my luggage upstairs and into my bedroom, the one he had designated mine since the day he moved in, and the one I stayed in every time I came to visit him. I threw myself on the queen-size bed and he lay next to me, grabbing my hand and holding it tight.

"I'm so happy you're here to stay, Anna."

"Me too." I glanced over at him with a smile.

"I hate to ask this, but have you talked to Matthew at all?"

"No. I haven't."

"You know that you need to put closure on this situation," he spoke.

"I know and I tried to call him, but he blocked my number. So then I went on his Facebook page and he blocked me there too. I called his office phone and Sam, his secretary, told me that he told her if I called, she is not to put me through. You're the only one who will understand why I did what I did. You're the only family I have left."

Franco Stiles and I had been best friends since the moment we laid eyes on each other in the ninth grade at boarding school. His six-foot stature, perfect black hair, and dreamy brown eyes captured my attention. I greeted him with flirty eyes, and right off the bat, he told me he was gay. Of course he was. After we graduated, we both attended Harvard University, where I obtained an MBA and he graduated with a bachelor's degree in Art. He was born with a gift and talent for fashion and was now the proud owner of Stiles Designs.

"Oh, by the way, I sold your dress." He smiled.

"You did?"

"I had a client come over and she took one look at it and had to have it. I only had to do a few alterations."

"You didn't tell her how the dress ditched the groom and ran away, did you?"

He let out a light laugh. "No. I told her I made it for a friend and the wedding got cancelled. So any idea what you're going to do now? Technically, you don't have to work, but I know you and you get bored very quickly."

"I was thinking about getting a job." I smiled. "Something simple."

"Like?"

"I don't know. I'll have to look online."

Franco looked at his watch.

"Shit. I have to run." He kissed my forehead before climbing off the bed. "I have an appointment at the studio. I'll be back later, and we'll order in."

"Sounds like a plan. I'm just going to get settled."

After he left, I unpacked and put everything away. I felt as if my life was in shambles, but at the same time, I felt free as a bird. I knew eventually this day would come. The day that my father would disown me. I tried to please him once I entered into adulthood, but when the bond between a father and daughter is never established, it's quite difficult. He would tell you that my little stunt at the wedding was just another cry for attention. I had done some pretty shitty things to get his attention back in the day and that landed me at boarding school in Connecticut, all the way on the other side of the country. So far out of his hair that he didn't have to deal with me anymore. I accepted it and was now grateful he sent me away or else I never would have met Franco. And from that day on, I never underestimated my father again.

I plopped myself down on the comfy black leather reclining couch, and as soon as I opened my laptop, my phone rang, and it was Franco.

"Hello."

"Thank god you answered. I got so swept up with you being there, I forgot my design book in my office. Would you be a doll and bring it to me? My client will be here in five minutes."

"Of course. I'll be there soon."

I grabbed my coat, put on my knit hat, grabbed his design book, and hailed a cab to his studio. When I walked inside, Franco was standing there talking with a woman who appeared to be in her early fifties.

"Thank you," he sighed as he kissed my cheek.

"And who is this lovely young woman, Franco?" The woman smiled.

"This is my best friend, Anna. Anna, I would like you to meet Jules Warren. I'm designing her wedding dress. One that is simple yet classy." He grinned.

"Nice to meet you, Jules." I smiled as I extended my hand.

"It's lovely to meet you, dear. I don't mean to be pushy or rude, Franco, but I'm on a bit of a time limit." She heavily sighed.

"What's wrong, Jules?" Franco asked as he flipped open his design book.

"I'm having trouble finding someone who's a perfect fit for one of my clients. His personal assistant is moving out of state and he isn't dealing with it very well. Her last day was today and his company hasn't found a replacement yet, so he called me to send someone over temporarily."

"Anna here is looking for a job and temporary is her thing." He smiled.

I shot him a look. Jules brought her index finger up to her lips as she looked me up and down.

"Hmm. Do you have corporate experience, darling?"

Franco walked over and hooked his arm around me.

"Are you kidding? Anna was the personal assistant to Clyde Baker of Baker Industries for years."

"Really?"

She seemed highly impressed.

"Yes. I was." I smiled through gritted teeth.

"Why did you leave?" she asked.

"Well—I've been wanting to move to New York for a while, so I took the plunge and here I am."

She reached into her purse and pulled out her business card.

"Here is my information. Email me your resume and references tonight and I'll be in touch after I receive them."

"I will definitely do that." I nodded.

## CHAPTER SEVEN

*Anna*

As soon as Franco walked through the door, I walked over and slapped him on his chest.

"How could you do that to me?"

"What? You said you wanted to get a job and the opportunity presented itself. Besides, it's only a temporary position. When you're done with that job, you can take some time off and then look again."

"How the hell am I supposed to provide a resume? The only company I ever worked for was my father's!"

"It's already taken care of, doll. I called my cousin, Lars. He'll be here in a while."

"Lars, the criminal?" I cocked my head at him.

"He's technically not a criminal." He rolled his eyes as he walked away and into the kitchen.

"Yes he is! He makes fake documents, IDs, passports, and god knows what else."

There was a knock at the door. Sighing, I walked over and opened it to find Lars standing there.

"Anna, baby. It's good to see you." He grinned as he lightly planted a kiss on each side of my face.

"Lars. Nice to see you. Come in."

"Franco told me you left your fiancé and moved to New York. Bravo, darling." He smiled. "Anyway, welcome, and this is for you." He handed me a large manila envelope. "It contains your resume and references."

I took it from him and removed the papers that were inside.

"Looks nice, Lars. And what if Jules calls Mr. Baker and he tells her he's never heard of me?"

"No worries, darling. It's all been taken care of. The number we put down for Mr. Baker is one of ours with a California area code. If and when she calls, my people will handle it along with your references. I've also sent that to your email so all you have to do is send it off."

"Gee, Lars, you did all this so quickly. Thank you," I spoke in a sarcastic tone.

"Quick is my specialty, and since you're a close friend of mine, I've decided not to charge you." He hooked his arm around me. "I take care of my friends."

I gave him a smile so fake, my face hurt. Grabbing my laptop and sitting down on the couch, I opened my email and forwarded my resume and references to Jules. Within a few minutes, she emailed me back.

*Anna,*

*It is my pleasure to offer you the personal assistant position we discussed. You will report to Carter Capital tomorrow morning promptly at eight a.m. I've listed the address below. I've also attached some forms I need you to fill out and sign for our company. Please remember that this position is temporary, and a permanent replacement can be found at any given time by Carter Capital. Please feel free to contact me with any questions or concerns you may have.*

*Jules Warren*

∼

The next morning, after showering and putting on my black pinstriped pant suit, I poured myself a cup of coffee and leaned up against the island. This wasn't what I had planned to do my first morning here in New York. Damn Franco for opening his mouth.

"Good morning. Oh, look at you. All business-like and ready to go." Franco grinned before kissing me on the cheek. "How did you sleep?"

"I slept okay." I twisted my face.

"I know that look, Anna. It's your bummed-out look. What's wrong?"

"Nah, it's nothing."

"Come on. Talk to me."

"I can't stop thinking about how my father fired me for not marrying Matthew." I took a sip of my coffee. "What parent does that to their child?"

"Working for your father was the only thing you've ever done that was expected of you. You could have worked anywhere after college, but you decided to stick with the family business because you knew it was the right thing to do. I'm sorry, darling." He hooked his arm around me. "But you weren't going back anyway, and you knew that."

"I know. But he didn't know that. Anyway, I'm off to work. Wish me luck personal assisting whomever it is I'm personally assisting."

"Probably some really old-ass dude who's going to sexually harass you." He smirked.

"You're probably right." I rolled my eyes.

## CHAPTER EIGHT

*Anna*

I stepped inside the tall building that was located at 100 Park Avenue and took the elevator up to the thirty-first floor. As soon as the elevator door opened, I was promptly greeted by a woman who looked to be in her twenties with long black hair and a massive amount of lip injections.

"Welcome to Carter Capital. How can I help you?"

"I'm Anna. Jules Warren sent me over."

"Hold please." She held up her index finger as she picked up the phone on her desk. "Follow me." She brightly smiled.

I followed her down the long hallway, past numerous cubicles and offices, until we reached the desk of a woman named Tori.

"Hi, you must be Anna. I'm Tori." She extended her hand.

"Nice to meet you, Tori."

"I'll show you to your desk. Mr. Carter is in a meeting right now down in the conference room, so I'll show you the ropes until he returns."

I gave her a pleasant smile. I was starting to think that maybe this wasn't a good idea. Oh wait. It wasn't my idea. But it was different, and it could be kind of fun. Plus, it was only temporary.

"Chrissy was extremely organized and she's going to be missed. She left step by step instructions for whomever took over." She picked up a piece of paper from the desk and handed it to me.

"Yes, she was very organized, but I do see a few things that could be modified."

"Mr. Carter won't like that. So please, just stick to the list. And remember, you're only a temp," she spoke in a snotty voice.

"Right." I gave her a fake smile.

I wanted to tell her who I was and what I really did. I took a seat behind my new desk, which felt weird because I wasn't used to working on this side of an office. The phones started to ring and I quickly answered them in the precise way that was on Chrissy's instruction sheet.

"Good morning, Carter Capital. Mr. Carter's office, this is Anna. How may I assist you?"

I took down message after message and stacked them neatly in a pile on the left hand side of the desk per my given instructions. I think Chrissy had OCD. I sat there and wondered when my old-ass boss was going to return. I'd already been here two hours and I had yet to meet him.

"Excuse me, Tori? Can you please direct me to the restroom?"

"Right around the corner." She smiled.

After I was finished, I walked back to my desk and Tori was standing there with her arms folded.

"May I help you?" I asked.

"You were in the bathroom approximately seven minutes, two minutes over the allotted five-minute bathroom break time."

I stood there and narrowed my eye at her.

"I apologize. I didn't know there was a time limit on bathroom breaks. Chrissy failed to mention that on her eagerly over-organized instruction sheet."

"Well, now you know. What were you doing in there for seven minutes?"

*Was she serious? This was going to be fun.*

"Well, if you must know." I smiled. "I was getting myself off."

She swallowed hard as she stared at me with a look of disgust on her face.

"Oh come on, Tori, don't tell me you've never—"

"Mr. Carter needs you to bring him a file to the conference room," she quickly interrupted as she picked up a file folder from the desk and handed it to me.

"Are you going to tell me where the conference room is?" I arched my brow.

"Down the hall, make a right, and it's conference room one." She hastily turned and scurried away. I laughed and headed to the conference room to meet the old man. When I approached, the door was shut, so I lightly knocked on it.

"Come in," I heard a voice speak.

When I opened the door, I went to take a step in and abruptly stopped as I stared at the man looking down at his phone. He looked up at me and had the same shocked expression across his face as I did.

"Wes?" I furrowed my brows.

"Anna?" He stood up. "What are you doing here?"

"Wes Carter? Carter Capital?"

"Oh no. Are you—"

"Your new personal assistant? Yes."

My belly fluttered and my lady parts started to spasm.

"You're not an old-ass man who's going to sexually harass me," I spoke. "You're my one night in Paris stand."

"What?" He chuckled.

"Nothing." I shook my head as I fully stepped inside the room.

He walked over to me and gave me a hug.

"It's good to see you again, but I'm totally confused as to what's going on," he said.

"It's good to see you too. Let me see if I can enlighten you. I'm your new personal assistant hired by Jules Warren."

"I didn't know you lived in New York."

"I just moved here, like yesterday."

"Didn't you just get back from Paris?"

"Yeah. Yesterday. It's a long story." I waved my hand in front of me.

"You seem to be the queen of long stories." He smirked.

"To be honest, my life is one big long story."

"If you just got back from Paris and you just moved to New York yesterday, how did you meet Jules?"

I let out a sigh. "It's a—"

"Long story. Right?"

"Yes."

"Something is off here." His eye steadily narrowed at me. "When I met you in Paris, you certainly did not seem like the personal assistant type. So this is what we're going to do. You're going to have dinner with me tonight and tell me all of your long stories."

"I am?" My brow raised.

"Yes. You are."

"Well, just so you know, I don't think going to dinner with the boss is a good idea. People will talk, and I'm pretty sure Tori already hates me."

He placed his hands on my hips and gave them a firm grip. Fuck. I lost my breath.

"Dinner with me is always a good idea." He grinned. "Boss or not, I'm picking you up at seven, so I expect your phone number and address sitting on my desk when I return to my office."

"You're awful bossy. I'm not sure I'm going to like working for you."

"You'll love working for me." He winked. "That I can promise you. Thanks for the file. I'll be heading back to my office shortly."

I gave him a smile, turned, and headed for the door.

"By the way," I said as I stopped and turned around. "If you're planning on reading my resume, don't. It's all a lie."

"You lied your way into this job?" His brow arched.

"I did." I smirked as I walked out the door.

## CHAPTER NINE

### Wes

As soon as she walked out of the conference room, a smile crossed my lips. I was in total shock when I looked up and saw her standing there.

"Hey, Wes, here are the numbers you requested," Christopher spoke as he entered the conference room.

"Thanks." I took the papers from him.

"By the way, have you met your new personal assistant. Fuck, she's smokin hot."

"Yes, I just met her. Her name is Anna." I raised my brow.

"Really? That's funny. Wasn't that the name of the girl you slept with in Paris?"

"That is the girl I slept with in Paris."

His brows furrowed as his jaw dropped.

"That girl? The one sitting outside your office is the Anna from Paris?"

"She sure is." I smiled.

"The one who left her fiancé at the altar and ran away?"

"Yep. That's her."

"Shit, Wes. Did you know she lived in New York?"

"She just moved here yesterday." I leaned back in my chair.

"And how did she get this job so fast?"

"She said it's a long story. A story she'll be telling me when I take her to dinner tonight."

"Damn. Well, okay. I guess this a good thing she's here, right? Or not?"

"It's good to see her again. I really enjoyed our night in Paris."

"Be careful, Wes. She may take these jobs as personal assistants to CEOs hoping to get her claws into them because she knows they're filthy rich."

∼

I finished up in the conference room and headed back. When I arrived at my office, I found Anna on the phone writing down a message. I pointed to my office and asked her to come in when she was finished. Taking a seat behind my desk, I noticed my phone messages weren't in the same spot they always were but sitting smack dab in the middle of my desk.

"You wanted to see me?" Anna asked with a smile as she stepped into my office.

"Yes. First, didn't Chrissy leave you a list of specific job instructions?"

"She did." She grinned.

"Then why are my phone messages sitting in the middle of my desk instead of slightly tucked under my phone?"

She brought her finger up and lightly tapped her lip as she glared at me.

"Perhaps I was wrong."

"Wrong about misplacing my phone messages?" I asked with an arch in my brow.

"No. Wrong about Chrissy having OCD. You're the one with OCD."

"I don't have OCD. I just like my messages neatly placed in the same spot they've been for years."

"Are you having anxiety because I didn't place them properly?"

"No," I spoke as I took my messages and put them in their proper place.

"Oh, I think you are." She smiled.

"Anna, stop. Please just place them here." I pointed to my phone. "Have a seat. We need to chat."

She sat down in the chair across from my desk and crossed her long legs. Images of those legs wrapped around my waist back in Paris came to the forefront of my mind and my cock started to twitch. I cleared my throat.

"I don't see your phone number and address on my desk like I asked. Do you have a problem following directions?"

"Obviously, you haven't checked your phone," she said.

I pulled my phone from my pocket and there was a text message with an address typed into it. I glanced up at her and a bright smile crossed her lips.

"How did you get my cell phone number?"

"From the phone on my desk. It was programmed under autodial number one."

I slowly shook my head with a smile on my face as I added her in my contacts.

"Excuse me, Mr. Carter." Tori popped her head into his office.

"Yes, Tori?"

"Human Resources sent this up for you," she said as she shot Anna a look.

"Thank you." I held out my hand and she handed me the file folder.

I glanced at Anna, who sat there with a grin on her face while she stared at Tori as she left my office. I opened the folder. It contained Anna's paperwork and resume.

"Anna Young. Nice last name." I smirked at her. "It says here that you were the personal assistant for Clyde Baker, CEO of Baker Industries in California. You're telling me that you made that up?"

"I didn't make it up. Franco did."

"And who is Franco?" I cocked my head.

"My best friend and roommate."

"You're living with a guy?" My eye slightly narrowed.

"He's gay. Long story. We go way back."

"Good. You can tell me all about it at dinner tonight. I would love to know how you scammed your way into my office."

"You make me sound like a criminal," she spoke.

"Are you?"

"No. You'll understand tonight. Now, if you'll excuse me, I hear the phones ringing out there."

She got up from her chair and walked to the door.

"Anna?"

"Yes." She turned around.

"Why does Tori not seem to like you?"

The corners of her mouth curved into a cunning smile.

"I may have told her I was getting myself off in the bathroom."

I sat there as my cock started to rise at her mere words and swallowed hard.

"We'll talk about that tonight," I spoke.

## CHAPTER TEN

*Anna*

The mere sight of him sent me straight into an orgasm. I had thought about that night in Paris every single day since it happened. I tried to forget about it and him, but I couldn't, and now, here I was working for the man I was never supposed to see again. I was dying to tell Franco, but this was something that had to be done in person, not over the phone or via text.

"I'm on my way to a meeting and I won't be back before you leave. I'll see you at seven." Wes gave me a wink as he walked past my desk.

"Enjoy. I'll be ready and waiting. By the way," I shouted. "My biggest pet peeve is lateness."

"Noted." He turned around and gave me a smile.

"What was that all about?" Tori strolled over to my desk.

"He's taking me to dinner tonight." I smiled a big fuck you at her.

"Why?"

Her snotty tone rubbed me the wrong way. I could have totally had fun with this one, but I did needed to remain professional. I didn't want any rumors started around the office, even though I was pretty sure she already told everyone what I said to her earlier about the bathroom. I actually needed to set the record straight with her.

"Listen, Tori. It's obvious you don't like me and I'm not sure why. What I told you about the bathroom earlier, I lied. After using the bathroom, I just kind of stayed in there a few extra minutes to think. I just moved to New York yesterday and I'm just feeling a little overwhelmed because this job happened so quickly. As for Mr. Carter, he's taking me to dinner to go over some work-related stuff and rules. That's it."

"I see."

"I'm sorry for what I said to you earlier. Can we be friends?" I extended my hand.

"No." She smiled as she turned on her heels and walked away.

*Bitch. Now it was game on.*

As soon as I entered the apartment and kicked off my heels, Franco came down the stairs and greeted me with a hug.

"How was your first day, Madame?"

"Well, there's a woman in the office named Tori who hates my guts."

"Really?" he asked with an expression of shock. "Who could ever hate you?"

"I could give you a list of people who hate me. But I do have something to tell you. I've been dying all day and couldn't wait to get home!"

"Did your old-ass boss sexually harass you?" he asked with excitement as he lightly grabbed my arm.

"He's not an old-ass. His name is Wes Carter. As in the sexy American I slept with in Paris."

"Shut up! No way. How is that possible?"

"Right? I was in total shock and so was he. Anyway, I have to go get ready. He's picking me up at seven and taking me to dinner."

"Goodie. I can't wait to meet him. Oh shit, Anna. You're going to have to eventually tell him that you lied to get the job."

"Already did. That's one reason he's taking me to dinner. He wants my full story."

"Believe me, darling, he wants more than that."

"I hope he does." I winked.

## Wes

My driver, Frank, pulled up to Anna's building and I climbed out of the car. There was no way she could afford a place like this on a personal assistant's salary. But then again, she did say she was living with her best friend. I walked into the building, told the doorman who I was, and took the elevator up to the eleventh floor. When I stepped out, I walked down the hallway until I found apartment 1120. After knocking on the door, it opened, and a man stood there and stared at me from head to toe.

"Well, hello there." He smiled. "You must be Wes. I'm Franco, Anna's bestie." He extended his hand.

"It's nice to meet you, Franco." I shook his hand.

"Please, step into our humble abode."

"Thank you." I stepped inside and looked around.

"Anna will be down in a minute."

"Your apartment is great," I spoke. "Do you mind if I ask what you do?"

"I don't mind at all. I'm a designer and I run and own Stiles Industries. In fact, I made Anna's wedding dress. Oops. Maybe I shouldn't have told you that. Oh well, she won't mind. Let me show you."

He grabbed his phone from the table and handed it to me. I gulped when I saw her picture.

"Wow. You made that?"

"I did and I made her veil. Isn't she delicious?"

"You're very talented."

"Thank you." He grinned. "I'm also designing Jules Warren's wedding gown."

"Really?" I cocked my head.

"Franco, what are you doing?" Anna asked as she walked down the stairs in a stunning black and silver short dress.

"Nothing." He grabbed his phone from my hand.

She shot him a look and then a beautiful smile graced her lips as she turned and looked at me.

"Hello. You look stunning." I grinned.

"Hi. Thank you. Are you ready to go?" she asked.

"I am. After you." I placed my hand on the small of her back. "It was nice to meet you, Franco."

"The pleasure was all mine, Wes. You two have fun."

## CHAPTER ELEVEN

*Anna*

Wes made a reservation for two at Le Bernardin. When we stepped inside the elite French restaurant, the young blonde hostess seated us at a quiet table in the corner for two.

"Good evening, Mr. Carter. May I start you and the lovely lady off with something from our drink menu?"

"Good evening, Enzo."

"I'll have a neat martini, please," I said with a smile.

"And I'll have the same," he spoke.

"So what did you think of Franco?" I asked.

"He seems very nice and I can tell he cares for you a lot."

"He's my best friend. Honestly, I don't know what I'd do without him." I picked up my glass of water and brought it to my lips.

"On a more serious note, tell me how you wormed your way into being my personal assistant? I'll be honest, Anna, I have trust issues when it comes to women and knowing that you sent in a fake resume raises some red flags for me."

I sat there for a moment and narrowed my eye at him. Okay. I could understand his concern.

"Well then, we both have something in common. You don't trust women and I don't trust men. But, if you want the truth, I had to run Franco's sketchbook over to his studio yesterday, and when I arrived, Jules was there. She was going on and on how she was on a time crunch because she had to find a replacement for you. Franco opened his big mouth and created the story of how I worked for Mr. Baker. Then, before I knew it, she gave me her business card and told me to send over my resume. So Franco had his criminal cousin, Lars, make a fake resume with fake references and I sent it over and she hired me. Trust me, I had no intention of getting a job so soon. It all happened so quickly."

He sat there with a narrowed eye and listened intently to every word I spewed at him.

"So then you don't have any personal assisting or office experience at all?" he asked.

*Moment of truth.*

"Oh no, I have a lot of 'corporate' experience. But I'm usually the one sitting in the big office with the personal assistant."

"What?" he asked with confusion.

Enzo brought our drinks and proceeded to take our dinner order. After he walked away, I took in a deep breath and extended my hand to Wes.

"I'm Anna Young, Chief Operating Officer of Young Vine Enterprises. I graduated from Harvard with an MBA and was valedictorian of my graduating class."

He slowly placed his hand in mine as a look of shock swept over his face.

"As in Young Vine Wines?" he asked.

"Yep. That's the one." I threw back my martini. "Except now, I'm just Anna Young. My father fired me because I didn't marry Matthew. In fact, he did it that night I was with you."

"I'm sorry, Anna. I don't understand. You're his daughter. Why would he do that? Why would he choose him over you?"

"If you knew my father, you would understand. It doesn't matter. I knew if I left Matthew standing at that altar, there would be no going back. He hired Matthew to groom him to be my right-hand man when he retired from the company. He took him under his wing and called him the son he never had. You know what, I need another martini."

"Of course."

Wes held up his finger, got our waiter's attention, and ordered two more martinis.

"Why are you taking a job as a personal assistant?" he asked. "You are so enormously over qualified."

"I didn't plan on it. Like I said, it just happened. I wasn't sure what I was going to do. But Franco knows I get bored easily, so he thought it would be a good idea since it was only temporary. Now, on to you, Mr. Carter. Why don't you trust women?" I grinned.

"I'm not finished asking the questions, Miss Young. So your father cut you out of the company completely?"

"Yep." I sipped my martini. "Technically, I quit. I knew the moment I got on that plane to Paris, I was done."

"But why? Didn't you like working there? If I recall, I read an article once about Young Vine and the company has been in your family for generations."

"You're right. It has been. I liked working there but not with my father."

"And what about your mother? What does she have to say about all this? I noticed you haven't mentioned her."

"I don't talk about my mother and for good reason. She's not a part of my life. She never has been, and she never will be."

"I'm sorry," he softly spoke.

"Don't be. She's a subject I don't talk about." I looked down as I could feel my eyes start to swell with tears.

*Damn it. I was stronger than this.*

Enzo walked over and set our plates down in front of us.

"Is there anything else I can get for you?" he asked.

"I think we're good, Enzo." Wes gave him a smile.

"Now it's your turn to answer some of my questions," I spoke.

"Fair enough. Go right ahead and I'll do my best to try and answer them."

Something told me he was going to pick and choose what he would and would not answer.

## CHAPTER TWELVE

**Wes**

"Wait. Before you start bombarding me with questions, I have one more," I said as I picked up my fork.

"Fine. One more it is." She smiled.

"Why don't you trust men?"

Her brow sexily arched as she stared into my eyes.

"Why don't you trust women?"

"I asked you first," I spoke.

"I'll tell you when you tell me."

"Well, I'm not ready to tell you. So I guess you can keep your secret as well. Besides me not trusting women, what else do you want to know?"

"Tell me about your childhood," she said.

"My father started Carter Capital a few years before I was born. My parents raised me with the intention that I would take over the family business when my father retired. Last year, on my thirty-first birthday, my father had a heart attack."

"I'm sorry, Wes."

"Thanks." I smiled. "It was pretty serious. He had to undergo a quadruple bypass and I took over while he was recovering. Once he was fully recovered, he told me that he and my mother talked about it and he was going to retire and leave me to run the company. He said his heart attack was a wakeup call and that he had a lot he wanted to do and see before he died. So my parents decided to travel the world and they have been doing it for the past seven months. In fact, I had just seen them when I was in Paris."

"Wow. Just the fact that your parents are still together is amazing," she said.

I let out a chuckle. "Yeah. I guess so."

"Let me guess. You're a Yale man."

The corners of my mouth curved upwards. "No. I graduated from INSEAD."

"In France?" she asked with surprise.

"Yes." I lightly laughed. "They have an excellent Executive MBA program."

"So I've heard. I've just never actually met anyone who has graduated from there. Congratulations, Mr. Carter." She held up her glass.

"Why thank you, Miss Young." I lightly tapped my glass against hers with a smile.

"So," she took the last sip of her martini, "why don't you trust women?"

"Why don't you trust men?" I raised my brow.

"Oh come on, Wes. Humor me. Tell me your dirty little secrets. I know you have some. There's no way a rich, corporate, sexy man like yourself is still single for a reason."

"Is that all that matters to you? Rich, corporate, and sexy?" I asked.

She studied me with a narrowed eye for a few moments as she brought her fork up to her mouth. She was trying to figure me out just like I was trying to figure out her. She had mommy and daddy issues big time. That much I could tell. She was gorgeous and very smart. But there was something off about her, and it was something I was going to find out.

"No. Maybe the sexy part." She smiled. "What's really important is what's inside. I like a man who is sweet, but not sickening sweet. I hate ass kissers. A man who works hard and isn't afraid to take risks. He must be sensitive, but not too sensitive. That's just fucking annoying. He must be kind and have a heart of gold."

"Was your ex all of those?" I daringly asked.

"He was just annoying all around."

I let out a chuckle as I slipped my credit card into the billfold. After I signed the receipt, Anna and I walked out of the restaurant and climbed into the back of my town car.

"When we get back to my apartment, would you like to come up? Franco made this amazing cheesecake for me and I have yet to cut into it." She smiled.

"I'd love to." I grinned.

When we entered her apartment, Franco didn't seem to be home. I took my coat off and set it down on the chair in the living room.

"Franco isn't here?" I asked.

"No. He's not coming home tonight."

"By the way, I forgot to say thank you for the present you left me in my suitcase." A smirk crossed my lips as I placed my hands on her hips.

"You're welcome. I thought it would be a nice memory of the night we had together. A little something to remember me by since we were never going to see each other again." Her arms wrapped around my neck.

"But look at us now." My lips softly brushed against hers. "We did see each other again."

"We sure did." She smiled.

"Shall we repeat the night we had in Paris?" I asked.

"Definitely."

She brought her lips to mine and my already semi-hard cock grew even harder. I couldn't wait to fuck her again. It was all I'd thought about since I'd been back in New York. I bent down and swooped her up in my arms, carrying her up the stairs.

"Which bedroom?" I asked as I broke our kiss.

"Last door on the left."

My hands gripped her hips as I thrust in and out of her from behind. Sexual moans escaped her lips as an orgasm tore through her. This was our fourth position and I'd held back as long as I could. I thrust one last time and held her against me as I exploded inside her, moaning with pleasure as my cock spasmed. I lowered my head and placed my lips on her shoulder as I tried to regain my breath. I pulled out of her and disposed of the condom while she climbed out of bed and slipped into her black silk short robe.

"Cheesecake?" She grinned.

"I'd love a piece."

"I'll be right back," she spoke.

# CHAPTER THIRTEEN

*Anna* My body was still on fire as the feeling of him still inside me radiated. I had never been so sexually fulfilled as I was when I was with him. I went into the kitchen, cut two slices of cheesecake, and took them back up to the bedroom. I handed Wes his plate and then lay across the bed on my stomach and faced him with my plate in my hand.

"So, tell me why you don't trust women." I smiled.

"You're cute." He tapped my nose with his fork.

"Then answer me this. Do you trust me?"

"Oh my god. This is the best cheesecake I've ever had."

"Right? Franco knows it's my favorite. He's quite a baker."

"Do you think he'll make me one?" Wes asked and I knew he was avoiding my question.

"If you ask him nicely. Now answer my question. Do you trust me?"

"No. Frankly, I don't."

"What? Why?" I cocked my head.

"Because you lied and sent in a fake resume."

"Please. I told you exactly who I was when I found out I was working for you." I pointed my fork at him. "I think I should get some points for that. I could have kept it a secret. But I didn't. I was honest."

"That is true. I guess I can give you a couple points for that." A smirk fell upon his face.

"Do I get extra points for sharing my cheesecake with you? I don't share with just anyone."

His eye steadily narrowed at me as the corners of his mouth curved upwards.

"Fine. I'll give you three extra points for sharing. But only because it's so damn good."

He set his empty plate on the nightstand and ran his finger across my lips.

"I better go. It's really late and we both have work in the morning."

"You can stay." I bit down on my bottom lip.

"It's tempting, but I won't have time to run home before the office in the morning."

"Okay."

Disappointment rose inside me because I remembered how good it felt with his body tightly pressed against mine as we slept that night in Paris. We both got up from the bed. While he got dressed, I took the plates down to the kitchen.

"I had a good time tonight," he spoke as his lips softly touched mine.

"So did I. Thank you for dinner."

"Thank you for dessert." He smiled. "I'll see you in the morning." His lips met mine one last time for the night.

"See you in the morning, Wes."

He walked out the door and I let out a sigh. I'd only been in New York for two days and I already had a job and slept with a man. The same man that I hadn't stopped thinking about since Paris.

The next morning, I stopped at Starbucks before work and grabbed myself and Tori a cup of coffee. Even though she didn't deserve it, I wanted to play nice on the playground.

"Good morning, Tori," I spoke with a smile as I set the coffee cup on her desk.

"What's this for?" she asked with a snotty tone.

"I stopped at Starbucks on the way in and thought you'd like a cup of coffee."

"I don't drink coffee, only tea."

She picked up the cup and handed it back to me.

"Noted." I graciously smiled as I walked away. "Bitch," I mumbled under my breath.

"Good morning," Wes spoke without even cracking a smile as he walked past my desk.

"Good morning. I brought you in a cup of coffee." I grinned.

"Thank you. I appreciate that. Come into my office so we can go over some things for today."

I followed him into his office and shut the door. I was hoping he'd at least give me a morning kiss, but he didn't. He just took his seat behind his desk and instructed me to sit down.

"Don't I at least get a kiss?" I smirked.

"Not in the office, Anna. I don't want rumors started."

"So are we just to pretend that there's nothing going on between us?"

He sat there and steadily narrowed his eye at me.

"There is nothing going on between us," he said. "We fucked a few times. That's it."

*Wow. Where was this coming from?*

"You're right. I didn't mean it any other way than that," I spoke.

"Every year, Carter Capital puts on an event for people who want to start a business to attend with the hopes of us investing in their company. We run an ad and accept the first one hundred people with a business plan who respond. We only choose one to invest in. I need you to start putting that event together. Chrissy should have a file in the cabinet by your desk with all the information. You need to book the venue and make all the arrangements for the food and put the ad together."

"Okay. That's great that the company does that for people."

"It's something my father started. It gives someone with a dream of becoming a business owner a chance in the community."

"I'll get started on it now," I spoke as I got up from my seat. "By the way, when is the event? Next month, two months?"

"Two weeks from tomorrow."

"Seriously? Why am I just finding out about this now?"

"Well, you've only worked for me for one day, and to be honest, I forgot about it until Christopher reminded me this morning. But I'm not worried. I know if anyone can put it together quickly, you can." He smirked.

"Damn right I can. Is that all?"

"Yes. Hold all my calls until further notice. I'm buried in paperwork I need to go over."

"Of course. By the way, do you want to grab some dinner tonight after work?"

"No. I can't. I already have plans," he spoke.

I walked out of his office and pulled opened the file cabinet, searching for the file Chrissy supposedly had. Found it. I pulled it out and took a seat behind my desk. Damn it. I wasn't the one who did this shit when I worked for my father. I always delegated this type of task. Picking up the phone, I dialed Franco.

"Hello, sweet cheeks," he answered.

"Franco, I need the person you use to organize your events."

"His name is Bernard. What do you need him for?"

"Wes is having me organize a business event and it's in two weeks. You know I don't really organize things myself."

"Ah, okay. Don't worry. I'll give him a ring right now and give him your number. I got you, babe."

"Thanks, Franco. I owe you big time. Oh, by the way, if Wes asks you to make him a cheesecake, tell him you're busy."

"What?" He chuckled into the phone.

"I'll explain later. Call Bernard now."

# CHAPTER FOURTEEN

## Wes

She walked out of my office and I felt nothing but conflicion. I felt like she was a woman I could get caught up in. A woman that I could fall instantly for. The woman I had already fallen for. And also a woman who had a lot of issues. Issues I wasn't about to take on. I needed to keep my distance from her and keep things professional for as long as she was my personal assistant. It was going to be hard and my cock wasn't going to like it, but I had no choice. I couldn't stand people who lied. I'd been burned before, and I would never let it happen again.

"Wes, you got a second?" Christopher asked as he popped his head in the door.

"Sure. Come on in."

"I have those reports you were looking for."

"Thanks, Christopher," I said as I held out my hand and he handed them to me.

He took a seat in the chair across from my desk and crossed his legs.

"Anna looks great sitting outside your office. She's one hell of a looker. How did dinner go last night?"

"It was good. She used to work at Young Vine Enterprises in California."

"The wine company?"

"Yeah. She was the chief operating officer and her father fired her after she ran off."

"No fucking way! What the hell is she doing being your personal assistant? Jesus Christ, she's probably more qualified to run this place than you or me."

"Apparently, she gets bored easily." I rolled my eyes. "I need to keep my distance from her."

"Why? I can tell you like her."

"I do, but I'm afraid I can't trust her."

"Why? Because she lied on a stupid resume? Big deal."

"I believe she's more trouble than it's worth. She left her fiancé at the altar. Her father fired her from the family business that she was supposed to take over, and her mother isn't in her life at all. What does that tell you about her?"

"It tells me that she comes from a shitty family," he spoke.

"Or it could be that she's the problem. I mean, I'm all for her knowing what she wants, but leaving that guy standing at the altar the way she did just isn't sitting right with me. If she didn't love him or was unsure, she should have called off the wedding. I just think she has some major problems and I'm not getting involved with someone like that."

"Is this because of Alexa?"

"No. This has nothing to do with her."

"I think you're wrong, man. I think this has everything to do with her and with what happened. Everyone has issues and nobody's perfect."

"I know that, and as much as I like Anna, I can't get involved with someone like her. It's too much. I'm at a good place in my life and I don't need any drama."

∽

*Anna*

I stood at the door and heard every word he said. My heart broke in half and I couldn't listen anymore. He didn't know me. He only knew what I chose to tell him. He didn't know anything about me or how I grew up. I walked back to my desk as I tried to hold back the tears that formed in my eyes. Picking up my phone, I sent Franco a text message telling him to cancel Bernard. I'd handle this event on my own and then I'd quit, and he'd never have to see me again.

I went through the file and the place where the event usually was held was booked. So I started calling around. I found a place, the Hudson Terrace, had an opening for the night of the event. Grabbing my coat and purse, I walked past Tori's desk.

"Mr. Carter is in a meeting. If he's looking for me, tell him I went to check out a space for the small business event."

"He isn't going to like that," she spewed.

"And I don't really give a shit." I kept walking.

As I was checking out the Hudson Terrace and speaking with the event manager, my phone dinged with a text message from Wes.

*"I don't understand why you had to leave. We have the event at the same place every year. All you had to do was make a simple phone call."*

I sighed as I rolled my eyes.

"Excuse me a moment," I spoke to Laurinda, the event manager. "My boss is being a dick head."

*"That place was booked already because you failed to plan this event more than two weeks ahead of time. I had to find somewhere else."*

*"Where are you?"*

"Don't worry about it. You wanted me to plan this and that's what I'm doing. I'll give you all the details tomorrow."

*"What's with the attitude?"*

"I don't have an attitude. I'm simply doing my job and you're interfering. Good bye, Mr. Carter."

I shoved my phone in my purse and continued talking to Laurinda. Once I signed the contract and picked the menu, I headed home, since my workday was already over an hour ago. Walking into my apartment, I set my purse down and fell onto the couch.

"Hey, welcome home. What's wrong?" Franco asked as he sat down next to me.

I slowly turned my head and looked at him with a look of sadness in my eyes.

"I overheard Wes talking to Christopher and he said some things about me."

"Like what?" He grabbed my hand.

"He said he thinks I have a lot of major issues because of my parents and the fact that I left Matthew at the altar, and he's not getting involved with someone like me. He said he's at a good place in his life and he doesn't need the drama."

"Aw, Anna. I'm sorry." He gently squeezed my hand and I laid my head on his shoulder.

"Christopher asked him if this had anything to do with Alexa."

"Who's Alexa?"

"I have no idea. I'm assuming an ex-girlfriend. She may be the reason why he doesn't trust women. The thing that sucks is I found myself falling for him. I mean, really falling for him. Like for real."

"You don't even know him, Anna."

"I know that. So explain to me why I couldn't stop thinking about him since Paris? We have this chemistry and I know he feels it too. I've never in my life felt like this about anyone."

"Not even Conrad Baines back in college? Because you were really into him."

"No. Not even Conrad. Like I said, this is different, and to be honest, it scares me. But I guess I don't have to worry about it anymore. He wants nothing to do with me."

"I don't think that's true. I saw the way he looked at you last night when you walked down the stairs and the way his eyes lit up. He just doesn't understand you, darling. He doesn't know what you've been through."

"You didn't hear what he said. So, it is true. I'm putting on this event and then I'm quitting.

"You'll figure it out." He kissed the side of my head. "You always do, and as for Wes Carter, I don't think this is over."

"Yes, it is. It's so over."

## CHAPTER FIFTEEN

### Wes

I sat in my study with my phone in my hand debating whether or not to text Anna. I didn't like our last conversation and her attitude bothered me.

"How was the venue you checked out?"

An hour later, a response from her came through.

"It was nice. I booked it. We'll discuss it tomorrow during office hours."

What the fuck did she mean 'during office hours'? Something was up with her and I wanted to know what it was.

"Need I remind you that you are my personal assistant and it's always business hours where I'm concerned?"

"LOL."

Did she seriously just laugh at me? I grabbed my coat and scarf and hailed a cab to her apartment.

"Wes," Franco spoke with surprise as he opened the door.

"Is she here?"

"Yeah. She's upstairs taking a bath. But—"

I pushed past him and walked up the stairs and into the bathroom that was connected to her room.

"Excuse me!" she yelled as I walked through the door.

"I've seen you naked, remember? What is going on with you?" I asked as I placed my hand in my pocket to tame my rising cock.

"Oh my god. Get out of here! Do you do this to all of your personal assistants?"

"Fine. I'll be waiting for you on the bed so we can talk about the event."

"I already told you that we'll talk about it tomorrow," she spat.

"No. I'm not waiting until tomorrow. So hurry it up."

I walked out of the bathroom, and as soon as I shut the door, I heard something hit it. To be honest, this wasn't me. I would never in a million years behave this way, but she got under my skin and I wanted answers. I sat down on the edge of the bed and waited for her. A few moments later, the bathroom door opened, and Anna emerged wearing her short black silk robe.

"Okay, you psycho. I booked a room at the Hudson Terrace. It can accommodate three hundred people, which is more than enough space. I arranged the appetizers and dinner will be served buffet style. It'll be easier that way and less formal. The less formal, the less nervous these small potential business owners will be. There's an area in the corner where I've arranged for a table to be set up for the owners to hand you their business portfolios and talk to you for a few minutes so you can get a feel for their character."

"I don't do it that way. I collect all the business portfolios and then me and Christopher go over them the next day. Whichever one we feel is the best fit is when we contact them and bring them into the office."

"Oh. Well, I like my way better. It's important to speak to each business owner directly."

"It's a waste of time if I'm not interested in their company."

"No. What's a waste of time is finding a business to help out and then finding out after the fact the guy is a dick head. That is a waste of time. You don't want to invest in a business if the owner is an asshole. This way, you can get a feel for someone and I'll be right there taking notes."

I sat and narrowed my eyes at her as she stood there looking sexy as fuck in that robe and her hair up in a messy bun.

"Fine. We'll do it your way," I hesitantly spoke. "Now tell me what's up with the attitude?"

"I don't have an attitude," she innocently spoke as she cocked her head.

"You do. I could sense it in your text message."

"Well, your senses are off, Mr. Carter. Now if you'll excuse me, I have things to do."

She started to walk past me, and I grabbed her hand and pulled her onto my lap.

"You have me to do," I spoke as I placed my hand between her legs.

"I don't think so."

"I do." I reached up and pulled the clip out of her hair and softly brushed my lips against hers.

"We can't," she moaned as my fingers stroked her.

"But we can. You're already wet because you can't stop thinking about my hard cock inside you."

Our lips locked and our tongues greeted each other with excitement. I broke our passionate kiss and looked at her just to be sure.

"Are you saying yes?" I asked.

"Just shut up and kiss me," she said as she pushed me down, straddled me, and removed her robe.

## CHAPTER SIXTEEN

*Anna*

Even while we were making love, I never once forgot what I'd overheard. My heart was still broken no matter how good he made my body feel. I needed to keep my heart out of it and let my body take over all the feelings. But it was hard. He was just another person in my life that thought I was more trouble than what it was worth. I could tell you that I was the love of Matthew's life, but I knew I wasn't. There were things Franco didn't even know. At first, I did believe he truly loved me, but as time went on, I knew he only wanted to marry me to get his hands into my family's company. Another reason why I left him standing at the altar. That was something I could never tell my father because he wouldn't believe it. He never believed anything I said, and as much as I tried to get proof, Matthew was very careful. Was I being paranoid because I believed no one could ever love me? No. There was something shady about Matthew.

"Oh my god," Wes moaned as he halted and exploded inside me.

He leaned down and kissed my lips before climbing off me and disposing of the condom. I sat up and slipped on my robe. As soon as he emerged from the bathroom, he slipped on his clothes.

"I'd stay, but you know I have that early meeting in the morning," he said as he gently swept the back of his hand down my cheek.

"It's fine. I didn't want you to stay anyway," I spoke as I got up from the bed.

"Oh. Okay."

"I'll see you tomorrow," I spoke, deadpan.

I followed him down the stairs and opened the door. He leaned in and gently brushed his lips against mine.

"Enjoy the rest of your night." He smiled. "See ya, Franco." He waved.

"Bye, Wes."

As soon as he walked out, I shut the door and walked to the kitchen.

"So much for it being over," Franco spoke as he followed me.

"It is. It's just sex."

"Not for you it isn't. You're emotionally involved."

"Not anymore. Not after what I heard."

"I'm confused as to why he came over here in the first place," he said.

"Because he wanted to know the details about the event and I wouldn't tell him. He's really OCD."

"Sounds to me like it was an excuse to see you."

"Just stop, Franco. I don't want to talk about Wes Carter anymore."

∽

The next morning, I went into the office and took a seat behind my desk to start working on the ad for the business event. Wes was in a meeting and I hadn't seen him yet, which was fine with me. Last night was the last booty call he was going to get. I needed to distance myself from him and keep things strictly professional. If I hadn't started putting this event together, I would have already walked out, but I felt this was important, especially for small business owners who were looking to make it big.

"Good morning. I'm back from my meeting," Wes spoke as he walked past my desk.

"Morning," I replied without even looking at him.

He stopped and I could feel his eyes staring down at me.

"Can I help you?" I asked as I looked up into his smoldering eyes.

"Are you okay?"

"I'm fine. I'm working on the ad for the event. Because you forgot and gave such short notice, it has to be in today."

"Sorry about that. When you're done, bring it in so I can check it over and then I need your opinion on something."

About an hour later, I finished the ad and handed it to him.

"This looks great." He grinned. "Have a seat."

I sat down in one of the chairs across from his desk and he handed me a file folder.

"What's this?"

"I want to know your thoughts about this company. Something isn't sitting right with me and I can't pinpoint what it is."

I opened the file and studied the proposal and numbers. After a few moments, I closed the file and handed it back to him.

"It's a lose/lose situation for you. I don't see where you would gain anything by investing in this company."

"That's what I'm thinking. Thanks." He smiled.

I got up from my chair and began to walk to the door. As I placed my hand on the handle, I turned and looked at him.

"By the way, about last night."

"What about it?"

"I asked you if you wanted to grab dinner after work, but you told me you already had plans. Then you show up at my place. Who's the liar now?" I arched my brow before walking out and closing the door behind me.

I took a seat behind my desk and my cellphone rang from a number I wasn't familiar with.

"Hello," I answered.

"Anna, it's Becca."

"Becca? How are you?"

"I'm fine. Listen, I need to talk to you," she spoke in a low voice.

"Okay. What's going on?"

"First of all, I wanted to give you a heads up. Your father is planning on buying back your shares of the company and giving them to Matthew, which would make him a forty-nine percent shareholder and partner."

"I'm not surprised. The two of them can do whatever they want. I want nothing to do with the company anymore or my father. If Matthew wants to buy my shares, then he can have them."

"Anna, you can't let that happen. Listen, I put in for a few days off. I need to see you. I told your father that I was going to visit my parents in Maine, which I am, but I need to see you first."

"What is going on, Becca?"

"I'll explain when I see you. Are you in New York?"

"Yeah. I'm staying with Franco."

"I figured as much. My flight gets in tomorrow morning at nine a.m."

"Okay. I'm working, but I can meet you here at the office."

"Where are you working?" she asked.

"Carter Capital. It's a long story. I'll ask Franco to pick you up from the airport and drop you off here."

## CHAPTER SEVENTEEN

*Wes*

"Excuse me, Mr. Carter," Tori spoke as she poked her head in my office.

"What is it, Tori?" I asked as I looked up at her.

"Can I come in for a minute?"

"Sure. Have a seat. What's up?"

"I just wanted to let you know that Anna has been on her cellphone for quite a while."

"Okay. What's your point?"

"I just don't think she fits in here."

"You're right. She doesn't fit in and let me tell you why. This position of being my personal assistant is beneath her. She's actually a former COO of a company in California. She has more experience and knowledge about running a company than perhaps me. So, if I were you, I'd be nice to her because you never know, you could be working for her someday."

She swallowed hard as she slowly rose from her seat.

"Yes, sir."

As soon as she walked out of my office, I pressed the intercom button and told Anna to come into my office.

"Yes," she spoke.

"There are a couple things I want to talk to you about, so sit down. First, I didn't appreciate that comment you made earlier about me being a liar, and second, Tori just came in here and told on you about being on your cellphone."

"Of course she did. As for calling you a liar, just admit it. And as for Tori, she can kiss my ass."

"We're not going to discuss about me lying to you right now, but personal calls should be saved for lunch."

"Well, it seems to me that you're running quite a tight ship here. Not that it's any of your business, but the call wasn't personal. It was a business call from one of my friends and VP at my former company. It seems that my father is going to try and buy back my shares of the company and give them to Matthew. She's flying in tomorrow morning to see me because there's something else she needs to talk to me about."

"I'm sorry to hear that about your father."

"Thanks, but don't be. Is that all?"

"Yes."

She got up from her chair and headed towards the door.

"I know there's more to all of this than what you're letting on. I have a hard time believing that your father is doing all this to you because you refused to marry some guy."

She stopped and turned her head.

"You really want to know the reason why?"

"Yes. Actually, I do."

"I was born. That's the reason." She turned away and walked out of my office.

I sat there with my hands folded and a narrowed eye as I stared at the door. What the fuck did she mean by that? I grabbed my phone from my desk and sent her a text message.

*"You're having dinner with me tonight at my place and we're going to talk."*

*"I already have plans."*

*"You're lying."*

*"As much as you would love to believe that I am, I can assure you I'm not.*

*Franco is hosting a pop-up event at a storefront space in midtown tonight and I promised I'd be there."*

"Oh. I apologize for thinking you were lying."

She didn't respond and I wasn't going to push it any further. As soon as she went to lunch, I called Tori into my office.

"You needed something, Mr. Carter?"

"Yes. Since Anna is at lunch, I need you to find out about a pop-up event going on tonight in Midtown. The designer's name is Franco Stiles. I want a time and an address."

"Yes, sir."

~

I left the office around six and headed home to change suits. All I could think about was last night. I vowed to stay away from her and keep things professional, but I blew it the moment I went over to her apartment. I couldn't help myself and I was finding that when it came to her, it was getting more difficult.

I arrived at the pop-up event, and when I walked inside, I looked around for Anna.

"Wes?" Franco smiled as he walked over to me. "What are you doing here?"

"Hi, Franco. I hope you don't mind."

"No. Not at all. Welcome to my pop-up event. Did Anna know you were coming?"

"No. Do you know where she is?"

"She's over there." He pointed to the corner of the space.

"Thanks." I patted his back.

As I walked over to her, she had her back turned and was holding up a beautiful black dress against her.

"I think you would look stunning in that dress," I spoke.

She froze and then slowly turned around.

"What are you doing here?"

"I've never been to one of these before and I was curious to see what it's all about."

"Okay. Enjoy." She smiled as she began to walk away.

I lightly grabbed hold of her arm and pulled her back to me.

"You're mad at me. Tell me why?"

"It's a long story." The corners of her mouth curved up into a cunning grin.

"Good, because I have all night."

"You really don't want to hear what I have to say to you. Besides, you're at a good place in your life and you don't need any drama. I'm more trouble than what I'm worth, Mr. Carter." Her brow arched before she yanked herself out of my grip and walked away.

*Shit. She must have overheard my conversation with Christopher. That explains it.*

She was standing by a rack of clothing when I walked up from behind and lightly gripped her shoulders with my hands.

"Then prove to me that you aren't," I whispered in her ear.

"I don't have to prove anything to you." She walked away and I followed her.

"Stop being stubborn, Anna."

She turned around as anger filled her eyes.

"We had one night in Paris and a couple New York nights. It was nothing but sex. Let's leave it at that."

"You overheard my conversation with Christopher. Admit it."

"You're right. I did, and you've expressed your true feelings about me to someone other than me." She walked out the door of the store.

"There are things you don't know about me," I said in a stern voice as I followed her out and grabbed her arm.

"And there are things you don't know about me either. You based your opinion on assumptions not facts. I heard you tell Christopher that I'm the one who had to be the problem, and you know what, in some ways, you're right." Her eyes began to fill with tears. "You don't have a clue what it's like not to ever be loved by your parents."

A single tear fell from her eye and I caught it with my finger before it had it chance to make its way down her cheek. I pulled her into me and held her tight as she struggled to get out of my grip.

"Let's go back to my place and talk," I spoke. "Please, Anna. Please just talk to me."

"No. I don't want to talk to you."

"I'm sorry. Please. We'll talk and that's it. I promise."

She lightly nodded her head.

"Let me go tell Franco that I'm leaving," she spoke. "I'll be right back."

"And I'll have the car brought around." I gently smiled at her as I wiped away another tear.

## CHAPTER EIGHTEEN

*Anna*

"Franco." I placed my hand on his shoulder.

"I know. You're leaving. I saw the two of you arguing. Go talk it out." He kissed my cheek.

"Are you mad?"

"Not at all, darling." He smiled. "I won't wait up for you."

"Thanks. I love you."

"I love you too."

As soon as I walked out of the store, Wes was waiting at the curb with the car door open. I climbed into the back seat and he slid in next to me. A nervousness settled inside me because I was about to tell him things I never talked about. He reached over and lightly grabbed my hand and interlaced our fingers together. I glanced up at him as a small smile graced his lips.

"I don't know about you, but I'm starving," he said. "How about I place an order for some food and have it delivered?"

"I'd like that. What did you have in mind?"

"Anything you want."

"There's a McDonalds right up there. We could order from the app and run in and get it."

"McDonalds?" A look of confusion swept over him.

"Yeah." I smiled. "I could really go for a Big Mac, fries, and a chocolate shake."

"McDonalds it is." He sighed.

When we pulled up to his Park Avenue building, he handed me the McDonalds bag and asked me to carry it along with my shake. I couldn't help but laugh.

"Are you embarrassed to be seen walking in with McDonalds?" I asked.

"Something like that." He smirked.

As soon as we stepped into the building, I couldn't believe my eyes.

"Miss Young?" Sebastian the doorman smiled.

"Sebastian? Oh my god. What are you doing here?"

I handed Wes the bag and my shake and gave him a hug.

"You two know each other?" Wes asked.

"We sure do. Sebastian was the doorman at my company. I had no idea you moved to New York," I spoke.

"I moved here shortly after I left. You knew I was originally from here."

"I know. It's so good to see you." I smiled.

"Still eating McDonalds, I see." He winked. "Are you here on business?"

"Umm. No. Actually, my father fired me, and I moved here. I'm staying with Franco until I find a place."

"He fired you?"

"Yeah. Long story." I waved my hand.

"You know how I always felt about your father. I'm sorry he did that to you. You don't deserve it."

"Thank you, Sebastian. Now that I know you're in New York, let's catch up over lunch some time."

"I'd like that, Miss Young. Enjoy your evening."

We stepped into the elevator and Wes inserted his key to the top floor.

"You better have been nice to Sebastian," I spoke as I opened the bag and took out a fry. "My father never was."

"I like Sebastian. I've never once been rude to him."

"Good. Because if I find out otherwise, you're going to have to deal with me."

He let out a chuckle.

When the door opened, an elegant marbled foyer greeted us, which led to an incredible spacious dining and living area that was decorated in muted grays and white. I followed him to the kitchen, which housed hand-painted cabinets in white, black Italian marble countertops, top-of-the-line appliances and an Italian marbled island that sat in the middle.

"Would you like to eat at the table or the island?" he asked.

"The island is fine."

I took a seat on one of the stools and Wes sat down next to me. Reaching in the bag, he pulled out my Big Mac and handed it to me along with my large fries. Taking the lid off my shake, I picked up a fry and dipped it in.

"That is disgusting," he spoke.

"Have you ever tried it?" I narrowed my eye at him.

"No, and I don't ever want to."

I popped it in my mouth with a smile, picked up another fry, dipped it, and held it up in front of him.

"You're making assumptions again, Mr. Carter. You can't do that until you know for a fact that you don't like it."

He sat there with a smirk across his lips as he took the fry from me and placed it in his mouth.

"Okay. I'll admit that it was pretty damn good."

I picked up my shake and placed it between us.

"Dip all you want." I grinned.

"Listen, Anna. I'm sorry for everything you overheard. I was just talking out of a place of confusion."

"Why? Because you like me but are afraid to admit it?"

"Something like that. I've told you before that I don't trust women, and this is the reason why. With my status and wealth, a lot of women are just interested in my money and what kind of lifestyle I can provide for them. It's happened numerous times over the years, and about three years ago, I met a woman named Alexa. We dated for a while and I liked her. I wouldn't say I loved her, but there was an attraction there. We had gotten into an argument one night and I told her that it wasn't working out and I didn't want to see her anymore. Just as I was about to walk out the door, she told me she was pregnant. To make a long story short, I did the right thing and married her and it turned out she was never pregnant. She faked the whole thing. We got divorced and she got a huge settlement that set her for life. It was a bad time in my life, and I don't like to talk about it."

"That's awful. I'm sorry, Wes." I placed my hand on his arm.

"Ever since her, I've been extremely cautious with whom I've dated. Nothing ever seemed to work out and I haven't found anyone worth trying for."

"Do you still talk to her?"

"No. She moved to Seattle and started a new life with my money, which I was grateful for. Because, honestly, I never want to see her again."

"You feel the way Matthew feels about me."

"Why did you do it, Anna? Why did you just leave him standing at that altar? I know there's something you're not telling me."

# CHAPTER NINETEEN

*Anna*

I sighed as I finished off my Big Mac, crumpled up the wrapper, and threw it in the bag.

"We need some drinks and a more comfortable spot for this story."

"What would you like?" he asked.

"A glass of scotch would be good."

"A woman after my own heart." He grinned. "Let's go into the living room."

He turned on the elegantly designed white fireplace and walked over to the bar that sat in the corner. I walked over to the double doors that led out onto a fabulously designed balcony that overlooked the Manhattan skyline.

"I like your place," I spoke.

"Thank you. Are you impressed?"

"No. Actually, I'm not." I smiled. "This is exactly what I expected you to live in."

He handed me my drink with a smile, took hold of my hand, and led me over to the couch.

"Matthew never loved me. He was using me."

"Using you how?"

"He was using me to get his hands into the company, only I couldn't prove it."

"Didn't you have him sign a prenup? Certainly your father wouldn't allow you to marry him without one."

"My father loved him like a son. They had this sickening bond, and when I suggested a prenup, he said it wasn't necessary and that I would offend Matthew if I even suggested it, so he told me to keep my mouth shut. I left him at that altar to spite both Matthew and my father. I wanted to embarrass the both of them. For once in my life, I wanted the upper hand. I wanted to make the decision and not have it be made for me. I didn't have a normal childhood like you did. You had two loving parents who loved you and wanted you. I had parents who couldn't even look at me."

"Anna," he softly spoke as he took hold of my hand. "What are you talking about?"

"After my mother gave birth to me, she went into a deep post-partum depression. She couldn't even bring herself to hold me and we never bonded. Even as I grew, she wanted nothing to do with me. I have memories of me at three years old begging her to hold me and she wouldn't. I remember walking into her room and all she'd be doing is sitting in her rocking chair facing the window and smoking a cigarette. My father hated it and they'd always fight. When I was five years old, he finally filed for divorce. He obtained sole custody of me and my mother was granted supervised visitations one day a week. At first, she didn't even bother to show, but then she sought treatment, and little by little, she tried to bond with me, but it still felt forced."

"I don't understand why she didn't seek treatment after you were born. Why the hell would she wait five years?"

"I don't know, Wes. I just don't. As I grew, she tried to keep in touch a little here and there, but I was so defiant at that point and I wanted nothing to do with her. I hated her for making me feel the way I did."

"And what about your father? How could he just stand there and let this happen?"

"My father." I laughed. "He resented me as well for my mother's depression. He blamed me. He didn't even want children, but she pressured him into having a baby. I grew up alone, except for the nanny that took care of me. I remember him sitting me down one day and telling me all of his expectations of me. I was a Young and I was expected to behave in a certain manner. He sent me to a private school from kindergarten on. He married my step-monster, Nina, when I was eight. She wasn't a fan of children, so we never got along. When I became a teenager, my defiance grew. I got caught smoking weed, shoplifting, and drinking. I'd do anything and everything I could to get my father's attention. Do you know that he never once told me that he loved me?" Tears formed in my eyes.

"Anna," Wes whispered as he put his arm around me and pulled me into him.

"I have never heard those words come from his mouth. He finally got fed up and sent me away to Choate Rosemary Hall, the boarding school in Connecticut, clear across the country so he didn't have to deal with me anymore. I was now their problem. I wasn't even allowed to come home for visits. That's where I met Franco and we've been best friends ever since. For Christmas, I would beg my father to let me come home, but he always said that he and Nina weren't going to be there because they were spending the holidays skiing in Aspen. He'd send me a Christmas card with a check in it for a thousand dollars and he wouldn't even sign it 'Love, Dad'; it was always just 'Dad & Nina.' So I went home with Franco for the holidays and spent it with his family."

"What about the summers?" he asked.

"Sometimes Franco and I stayed in Connecticut or I went home with him. Then we graduated and went off to Harvard. I was an independent woman who was planning for her future and I made a plan. I got back in the good graces of my father, proved that I was good enough to run his company, and after I graduated, I moved back to California, where my father made me the COO of Young Vine Enterprises. But I never underestimated him again, and I was always one step ahead."

"When was the last time you spoke to your mother?"

"I haven't spoken to her in years. She would try to call or come visit, but as far as I was concerned, she lost that right. Want to hear something funny? She's remarried with two children. They're the perfect happy family."

"Anna, I'm so sorry."

"Don't be, Wes. They made me who I am today, and believe it or not, I'm grateful for that. I'm a hard-working independent woman who doesn't need anybody."

"Everybody needs someone," he spoke as he kissed the top of my head.

"Maybe some do, but I don't."

"I'm sorry for making assumptions," he said. "I should know better."

"You should." I lifted my head and gave him a smile. "But you have trust issues and rightfully so."

"Still, I never should have said what I did. I'm truly sorry." He placed his finger under my chin. "I hope you can forgive me."

"I think I can."

"I admire you, Anna Young. I admire your strength and everything you've endured. I can't even imagine growing up like that."

"Thank you, Wes. I have a question for you."

"What is it?"

"Are you going to kiss me? Because I really feel the need to have your lips on mine." I grinned.

"I'm definitely going to kiss you." He leaned down and brought his mouth to mine. "And if you don't mind, I'm going to do more than that to you."

"I don't mind at all."

## CHAPTER TWENTY

*Wes*

I carried her up the stairs and to my bedroom, where I made love to her multiple times during the night. After everything she told me, I now understood why she did the things she did. She was so strong yet broken inside. Things in my mind became much clearer now that I knew more about her. She wasn't after me for my money. She had her own. She liked me for who I was as a person and not just the material things I could offer her.

She lay her head on my chest as she soundly slept and I softly stroked her hair. Was this the girl I'd been waiting for my whole life? I asked that same question that night in Paris because I felt something I'd never felt before when I was with her. But I'd never see her again, and yet, she was here, in my bed in New York City.

∽

"It's time to get up," I quietly spoke as I pressed my lips against her shoulder.

She rolled over and greeted me with a warm morning smile. "Do we have to go to work today?"

"Yes, and don't forget your friend is coming in."

"Oh shit!" She quickly sat up. "I did forget. I have to get home and change clothes."

"Relax." I grabbed her hand as she tried to bound out of bed. "We have plenty of time. Let's take a quick shower and then we'll head to your place on the way to the office."

"We'll be late and if we walk in together, people will talk."

"Then let them talk. I don't care."

We took a shower that lasted longer than I anticipated, but it was well worth it. After we got dressed, we headed back to Anna's place.

"Well, well. Good morning, Sunshines." Franco grinned as we walked through the door.

"No time to chat, Franco. I have to hurry and change," Anna spoke.

"Coffee?" Franco asked me.

"Sure. Do you have to-go cups?"

"I do." He slyly smiled. "Everything good between you two?"

"Yeah. Everything is good." I smiled. "She told me about her childhood last night."

"Pretty brutal, right?"

"I can't even imagine," I said. "What her parents put her through was awful."

"I'm ready," Anna spoke as she flew down the stairs.

"Your coffee, Madame." Franco smiled as he handed her the to-go cup.

"Thanks. You're a lifesaver." She kissed his cheek. "Don't forget about Becca."

"I haven't forgotten about her. I'm actually heading to the airport soon."

We were an hour late to the office, and when we walked in, all eyes turned to us.

"Good morning, Mr. Carter," Tori said.

"Good morning, Tori. Aren't you going to say good morning to Anna?"

She cleared her throat.

"Good morning, Anna."

"It's more than a good morning, Tori. It's a fabulous morning." She grinned.

Anna took her seat behind her desk and I walked into my office. As soon as I got settled, Christopher walked in.

"I saw you and Anna walking in together. An hour late, may I add." He smirked.

"We had a good talk last night. I told her about Alexa, and she told me about her childhood."

"That's good. So now what?"

"I guess we're going to see where things go."

"Alright. I'm happy to hear that. These contracts need your signature. As soon as you sign them, the Bradford property will belong to Carter Capital."

"Thanks, Christopher."

I had just gotten off the phone on a conference call when Anna walked into my office.

"Here are your messages," she said as she handed them to me.

"Come here." I smiled as I held out my arms.

She walked over and took a seat on my lap, wrapping her arms around my neck.

"You are the sexiest personal assistant I've ever had." I kissed the tip of her nose.

"And you are the sexiest boss I've ever had."

"Is Becca here yet?" I asked.

"She's on her way. To be honest, Wes, I'm a little nervous to hear what she has to tell me."

"No matter what it is, you can deal with it. I would be more than happy to sit in with you."

"I'd like that if you have time."

"Even if I didn't, I'd make the time for you." I placed my forehead against hers.

"Excuse me, Mr.—Oh my god. I'm sorry," Tori spoke as she closed the door in embarrassment.

"Busted." Anna smiled.

"Who cares. I know you'll set her straight." I kissed her soft lips.

## CHAPTER TWENTY-ONE

*Anna*

I walked out of Wes' office and glanced over at Tori's desk, where she was giving me the evil eye. I rolled my eyes and sat down at my desk. A few moments later, I saw Becca walking down the hall.

"Becca!"

"Anna. It's so good to see you again."

We gave each other a hug.

"It's good to see you too."

Becca looked at my desk and then at me.

"So what's your position here?"

"Don't laugh. I'm the CEO's personal assistant."

She laughed anyway and placed her hand on my arm.

"Stop it, Anna. You are not."

"Actually, I am. It's just a temporary thing."

"Hello," Wes said as he walked out of his office and extended his hand to Becca. "You must be Becca. I'm Wes Carter, Anna's boss."

She placed her hand in his and looked him over from head to toe.

"Well, hello, Mr. Carter. It's a pleasure to make your acquaintance." She grinned.

"I think the two of you will be more comfortable in the conference room. Follow me."

"Oh my god," she mouthed as she gripped my arm. "Tell me you've slept with him?"

A smile crossed my lips as I nodded my head. We entered the conference room and the three of us took a seat.

"I told Wes he could join us. He knows about Matthew and my father."

"Oh. Okay."

"So what's going on?" I asked.

"Do you remember signing off on some invoices from MJB Supplies?"

"Yeah. They're a new vendor that Matthew found about a year ago. I signed the first few and then he asked if I could just give him the authority to sign off on them because I was so busy doing other things. Why?"

"He's been signing off on other invoices lately. New vendors, distributors, and a PR Firm."

"Did you or Frank confront him?"

"I did, and he told me that the company is changing with the times and upping it's strategy. He said he and your father had a meeting about it and your father was on board. He also said that he and your father talked about reorganizing the company and certain positions would be cut out. And if I were to question his authority again, he would make sure my position was eliminated."

"Did you tell my father that he pretty much threatened you?"

"No. You of all people know how much that asshole means to your father. Frank and I wanted to come to you first, especially since we overheard that he wanted to buy back your shares and give them to Matthew. Anna, something shady is going on."

"It sounds to me like Matthew might be embezzling money from the company," Wes said.

"That's what I was thinking too." I glanced over at Wes. "But it's really not my problem, Becca. My father fired me."

"I know, and trust me, everyone is highly upset over that. But you still are a part of that company, and if anyone can do something, it's you. You know we can't go to your father with this. Not without proof. We'll all lose our jobs."

"Okay. I'll need to see the invoices that he's signing off on."

"Frank said you'd want them."

She reached into her bag, pulled out a file folder, and slid it to me.

"Thank you for meeting with me, Anna. I need to head back to the airport. I have a flight I have to catch to Maine."

"I'll have my driver drive you," Wes spoke.

"Why thank you, Mr. Carter. Oh, Anna, by the way, have you seen YouTube?"

"No. Why?" I narrowed my eye.

"I'll send you the link." She gave me a hug.

After walking her down the hallway and saying goodbye, Wes and I stepped into his office.

"I think you're going to need someone's help with those invoices," Wes spoke.

"I know just the person who can help me." I smiled.

"Who?"

"Criminal Lars."

"The one who made your phony resume?"

"Yep."

I pulled out my phone and sent Franco a text message.

*"Can you please send me Lars' phone number? I need his help."*

*"Of course? What's going on?"*

*"I'll explain later."*

Just as I was sending Lars a text message, an email came through from Becca. When I opened it, I placed my hand on my forehead.

"What's wrong?" Wes asked.

I handed him my phone and watched the reaction on his face as he watched the video of my wedding and me running up the aisle with a wide grin across my face.

"Look at that." He chuckled. "This video got over two million views. You're a YouTube sensation."

"Shut up!" I grabbed the phone from his hand, and he let out another chuckle.

"If it makes you feel better, you looked beautiful." He smiled.

Later that evening, Wes and I went to my apartment and waited for Lars while I explained to Franco what Becca had told me.

"I knew that guy was a snake," Franco spoke.

There was a knock at the door, and when I opened it, Lars gave me a tight hug.

"Hello, baby doll. Somehow, I knew you'd be needing me again." He grinned.

"Lars, this is Wes Carter. Wes, this is Lars."

"Nice to meet you, Lars," Wes spoke as he extended his hand.

"Trust me. The pleasure is all mine, Wes." He winked before placing his hand in his.

"He's my boss. You know, the one for whom you made me the fake resume?"

"Oh shit. She is wonderful, though, right?" He grinned.

"She certainly is," Wes replied.

"So what do we got?"

"I need you to check out these invoices, find out if these companies are real or shell companies, and then trace these account numbers."

"Is someone being bad and fraud-ing a company?"

"We suspect my ex-fiancé is," I replied.

"Oh. The one you left at the altar? By the way, what a beautiful escape. I saw the video. You should be so proud." He grinned from ear to ear as he placed his hand on my arm.

"How long is this going to take?" I asked with irritation.

"Perfection takes time, darling," he spoke as he set up his high-tech laptop on the table.

"I thought quick was your specialty?"

"It is, and if you were to give this to anyone else, you'd wait hours, maybe even days. I'll need about an hour. So go about your business and let me do my work."

"You don't by any chance have any cheesecake left, do you?" Wes asked with a smile.

"I do. Would you like a piece?"

"I would love a piece."

I went into the kitchen and took the cheesecake from the refrigerator. After cutting a slice, I brought it over to the couch where Wes was sitting.

"Thank you." He kissed my lips.

"Hey, Anna, it looks like your ex is a thief."

"You found something?" I asked as I got up from the couch and walked over to where Lars sat.

"All these invoices are fake, and these businesses are all set up as shell companies. Basically, they don't exist, and if they don't exist, they can't provide services. Now I've traced the account numbers to offshore accounts in the Cayman Islands all registered to Matthew James Bondi. Oh look, MJB Supplies. Coincidence? I don't think so." His brow arched.

"How much does he have in the accounts?" I asked.

"Well, darling, that's going to take a little bit of time for me to hack into them."

"Then get hacking!"

About thirty minutes later, Lars called me over. Wes and I got up from the couch and walked over to the table.

"Can I just say that I'm so happy you ditched that little thief," Lars said. "Between the four accounts, he's stolen over a million dollars of your daddy's money. Look, all of the money transfers came from Young Vine Enterprises."

"Damn him. Is there a way to transfer all that money out of his accounts and back into the company?"

"Darling, if I did that, then he'll know we hacked into his account, which is illegal."

## CHAPTER TWENTY-TWO

*Anna*

I packed an overnight bag and Wes and I headed back to his penthouse for the night.

"I really don't want to deal with all this," I spoke as my head rested on his chest. "To be honest, it's not my problem."

"He didn't just steal from your father, he stole from you too. You're still a part of that company until you sign papers that say otherwise. Don't forget that. Do you really want to let him get away with what he's done? I know you're thinking right now that your dad deserves it for trusting him so much, but this affects you. You need to fight for what's yours. Look at me, Anna."

I lifted my head from his chest and stared into his eyes as he ran his finger across my cheek.

"Wouldn't it give you great pleasure and closure to let your father know that the man he invested time in and chose over his own daughter screwed him over?"

"It would." I smiled.

"Then that's why you need to go back to California and tell him."

"I suppose you're right."

"Good, we'll fly out tomorrow."

"We?" I asked.

"You really don't think I'd let you go alone, do you? I'll admit, I'm anxious to meet the man who hurt the woman I—" He paused.

"You what?" I asked.

"I think I'm falling in love with."

The corners of my mouth curved upwards as I reached up and softly brushed my lips against his.

"I think I'm falling in love with you too."

"Really?" He smiled.

"Yeah. Really."

His grip on me tightened as our lips locked in a passionate kiss.

The next afternoon, Wes rented a private jet that flew us to California. I sat in the seat by the window and stared out as the plane sifted through the clouds.

"Are you okay?" he asked.

"Not really. I don't want to see my father or Matthew."

"I know you don't, but don't forget, they made you who you are today. A strong, independent woman. I'll be right there with you. If anything happens, I have your back." He brought my hand up to his lips.

"Thank you." I glanced at him with a small smile upon my lips.

We landed in L.A. and climbed into the car I had waiting to take us to the Four Seasons Hotel.

"It's nice to see you again, Miss Young," Xavier spoke.

"Thank you, Xavier." I smiled.

"Here is your room key to the Presidential Suite. I will have your bags brought up. As always, it's a pleasure having you stay with us." He nodded.

"How often did you stay here?" Wes asked with an arch in his brow.

"Enough." I grinned. "I actually lived here for a while after I graduated college. There was no way I was moving back in with my dad and step-monster."

We entered the Presidential Suite and Wes was kind enough to tip the bellhop who brought up our bags.

I sat down on the couch for a few moments to collect my thoughts before heading over to the company, because once I got there, the war would have begun.

"Are you having second thoughts?" Wes asked.

"No. I'm just preparing myself."

"Do you need sex first?" He winked.

A smile crossed my lips.

"I think you gave me exactly what I needed this morning, Mr. Carter."

"Okay. Just asking."

We left the hotel and climbed into the black sedan at the curb. When we entered the Young Vine Enterprise building, Roland, the security guard, stopped me.

"Anna," he spoke. "What are you doing here?"

"I'm here to see my father, Roland."

"You've been banned from the building."

"Of course I have." I smiled. "This is really important."

He took hold of my arm, looked around, and walked me over to the corner.

"Your father isn't here. He and Mr. Bondi are at a golf outing and won't be coming back. Your best bet is to catch him at home."

"That's right. It is that time of year for the annual golf outing. Thanks, Roland."

"I just want you to know you did the right thing. I don't like that Mr. Bondi."

"I don't either." I smirked. "Come on, Wes. It looks like we're paying a visit to my childhood home." I sighed.

The car drove up the long winding driveway and pulled up in front of the Young Mansion.

"How do you know when your father is going to be home?" Wes asked.

"He'll be here in a couple of hours. He and Matthew will walk through the door, laughing like they always do and then they'll go into the living room for a drink until Clarissa tells them dinner is ready."

"And what about your stepmother?"

"Nina is most likely at the spa like she always is when there's a golf outing."

We walked up the paved steps that led to the front door. Placing my hand on the handle, I took in a deep, cleansing breath. Opening the door, we stepped inside the large marbled space with the oversized Persian rug Nina bought when they were on vacation in Peru. I always hated that rug.

"Oh my gosh! Anna." Clarissa smiled as she emerged from the kitchen holding out her arms.

"Hi, Clarissa. It's good to see you."

"Oh my. I've missed you." She placed her hands on each side of my face.

"Clarissa, this is Wes Carter. Wes, this is Clarissa. She's been with us since I was a child."

"It's nice to meet you, Mr. Carter."

"And you as well, Clarissa."

"Anna, does your father know you're here?" she asked with a concerned voice.

"No, and I don't want him to. I want to see the look on his face when he sees me. Where's the step-monster?"

"Mrs. Young is at the spa. She'll be joining your father and Mr. Bondi for dinner."

"Told you." I smiled at Wes.

"Anna," she took hold of my hand, "your father is very angry."

"I know he is and he's about to get a whole lot angrier."

"Oh dear lord." She made the sign of the cross. "Can I get the two of you anything?"

"No. We'll just help ourselves to the bar."

"Very well. If you need anything, just ask."

I led Wes into the living room and walked over to the bar.

"Neat martini?" I asked him. "We're going to need it."

He let out a chuckle. "Sure."

I made the martinis and took them over to the couch, where I handed Wes his. As we were talking, the front door opened, and I heard the voices of my father and Matthew. Instantly, my stomach felt sick. I took in a deep breath as I looked at Wes.

"What the hell are you doing here?" my father asked as they walked into the living room.

The look on both of their faces was priceless.

"Hello, Dad," I spoke. "Matthew."

"You have some nerve showing up here," Matthew spoke. "If you came here to beg for my forgiveness, you can forget it. I will never forgive you for what you did."

"Please, get over yourself. You aren't worth begging for forgiveness from."

"Anna, I'll ask you one last time, what the hell are you doing here?" my father commanded.

"I need to talk to you about the company."

# CHAPTER TWENTY-THREE

*Anna* "The company is none of your concern anymore. In fact, I'm glad you're here. I have papers for you to sign. I'm buying back your shares of the company. Don't even try to fight me on it, because in the contract, I made sure to include a buy-back clause."

"Who is this guy?" Matthew harshly asked as he pointed to Wes.

"This is Mr. Westin Carter. I picked him up in Paris while I was on our honeymoon." I smirked.

"Why you—"

My father put his hand up.

"Stop, Matthew."

"Dad, I need to talk to you in private."

"I have nothing to say to you, Anna."

I sighed. "Okay, then. I guess we'll just hash it out right here. There's an employee in the company who is embezzling money."

"That's ridiculous. Nobody that works for me would ever do that. And how do you know this?"

"Yeah, Anna?" Matthew nervously chimed in. "How do you know this?"

"I was tipped off by one of your concerned employees, Dad."

"Who?" Matthew angrily shouted.

"Why are you getting so worked up, Matthew?"

"What is going on in here?" Nina asked as she walked into the room. "What is she doing here?"

"Hello, Nina." I grinned.

"That's your stepmother?" Wes asked.

"Shut up." I slapped his chest.

"She's here on business, Nina. Go see if dinner is ready."

"What business could she have? She doesn't work for the company anymore. Clarissa will let us know when dinner is ready."

"Anyway!" I loudly voiced. "Since Matthew won't fess up about embezzling money from the family company, I guess I'll just have to show you, Dad."

"What? You think I'm the one?" Matthew nervously laughed.

"Anna, you've gone too far this time," my father shouted. "First you broke this man's heart and humiliated him in front of our family and friends and now you stand there and accuse him of stealing from me?"

"Damn right I do." I reached into my bag and pulled out the file. "Here are all the bogus invoices he created and signed off on for services and supplies that the company never received. And these are the account numbers to which the company deposited the funds. The account numbers were traced to a few offshore accounts in the Cayman Islands, with over a million dollars total. A million dollars of your money, Dad."

He hastily grabbed the file from me and thumbed through the invoices.

"I've never even heard of these vendors." He looked at Matthew. "Why wouldn't you have run these by me first?"

"I—I didn't want to bother you. They're legit companies. I checked into them myself," he nervously spoke. "I would never steal from you. I can't believe you're standing here believing what she's saying. Especially after what she did to the both of us."

I stood there and rolled my eyes.

"Maybe you should have him check his accounts," Wes leaned over and whispered in my ear.

"Don't worry, Dad. I had the money transferred out of those accounts and placed back into the company account."

"What?!" Matthew shouted as he pulled out his phone and started typing away.

"Matthew?" My father cocked his head at him and then grabbed his phone from his hand. "What the hell?"

"What is it, Dad? Did someone get caught with their hand in the cookie jar?" I smiled.

"YOU BITCH!" Matthew came at me and Wes stepped in front of me.

"I suggest you back the fuck up now," Wes sternly spoke.

Matthew stopped and then turned and looked at Nina, who was slowly walking out of the living room.

"Oh no you don't, Nina. If I'm going down, you're going down with me. This was all your idea!" he shouted.

"Oh shit." I laughed. "I didn't see that one coming."

"Neither did I," Wes spoke.

Suddenly, there were police cars with their sirens and flashing lights in the driveway. Clarissa opened the door and two police officers stepped inside and handcuffed Matthew.

"Take her too. She was a part of this," my father spoke to the officers. "How could you, Nina? How could you do this to me after everything I've given you?"

She just stared at him as the officers hauled her and Matthew away. My father stumbled into the wing-backed chair and placed his face in his hands. I wished I could say that I felt sorry for him, but I didn't. This was his punishment for the way he treated me since the day I was born.

"How did you know, Anna?"

"I didn't know about Nina, but Becca paid me a visit in New York. She and Frank suspected something was up."

"Then why didn't they come to me? Why the hell would they go to you?"

"Because they knew you would never believe them. Plus, when Becca confronted Matthew, he gave her some spiel about how the two of you talked and wanted to take the company in a new direction. And then he threatened to fire her. Becca had no choice but to come to me."

"How on earth did you find out about those accounts?" he asked.

"I'm not at liberty to say. But I knew I had to put a stop to it."

"Thank you, Anna."

That was the first time I'd ever heard those words escape my father's lips.

"Don't thank me. I didn't do it for you. He was stealing from me too. My work here is done. Come on, Wes, let's go."

"Anna, wait," my father said. "I'm sorry."

"Sorry for what? Never being a father to me? Never loving me? Never trusting in me enough to make the right decisions for myself? Sorry that I was ever born?"

"Stop it!"

"No, Dad. I won't stop it. Because all of it is true. You chose to love and trust a man more than your own daughter and that is something I can never forgive you for," I spoke as tears filled my eyes.

"Anna, don't do this."

"It's too late, Dad. This can't be undone. There's too much damage. Send the papers to Franco's apartment in New York. That's where I'm staying. I'll sign over my shares to the company."

"No!" He stood up. "You are my daughter and part of that company belongs to you."

"I was never your daughter, Dad." I wiped my eyes and walked out.

# CHAPTER TWENTY-FOUR

## Two Weeks Later

*Wes*

Anna and I walked into the room at the Hudson Terrace and I could say that I was highly impressed. She did an excellent job of getting everything organized and set up.

"This looks great, Anna."

"Thanks. Actually, it was kind of fun. I think I like being on the other side of business things."

I gently kissed her lips and then walked over to Christopher, who was grabbing a drink at the bar.

"Anna did a good job." He smiled.

"She sure did. I'm very proud of her and I love her."

"That's great, man. I'm happy for you. Who would have thought that your one-night stand in Paris would become the love of your life?"

"I know." I laughed. "It's weird how things work out sometimes."

People started to pile inside the room and I walked up to the microphone and welcomed everyone and gave a short speech. Anna and I walked over to the buffet, grabbed some food, and then took our seats at the table where she had arranged for me to meet with the hopeful candidates that I would invest in their company.

"Hello, I'm Wes Carter."

"I'm Francine Lutz. Cupcake?" She smiled.

"Oh. I love cupcakes." Anna grinned as she reached over and took one. "These are beautiful. Did you bake them yourself?"

"Yes," she shyly spoke. "Cupcakes are my life and I've always wanted to open a cupcake store. I had been saving money for a couple of years and then my husband left me for another woman, and he stole the money I had saved."

"Oh. I'm so sorry," Anna spoke as she reached over and placed her hand on hers. "Well, let's taste these beautiful-looking cupcakes. Holy shit. These are the best cupcakes I've ever had. Oh my god, Wes. Try this." She shoved the cupcake in my face.

"Yes. It is very good," I spoke as I took a bite.

"What is in this frosting?" Anna asked.

"It's a family secret." She giggled.

She was a homely-looking woman who appeared to be in her late thirties with pin-straight long brown hair, thick bangs, and large black-rimmed glasses that looked too big for her face.

"Oh. I love those family secrets." Anna smiled.

"My ex-husband put together this business plan for me a couple of years ago when I talked about wanting to open up a shop. Then he laughed at me and said nobody would want my stupid cupcakes and he told me good luck. He crushed my dream. But I still had a vision."

"Well, thank you, Francine. I'll look this over."

"Thank you, Mr. Carter. I appreciate it. Would you like to have the rest of these cupcakes?"

"Yes! We'd love them!" Anna spoke in excitement. "Thank you, Francine."

I glanced over at Anna as she shoved another cupcake in her mouth.

"What?" she asked.

I laughed as I shook my head at her. When the event ended, we headed back to Anna's place so she could grab some clothes since she was spending the weekend at my place.

"I think you should invest in Francine's cupcake business," she said as we walked into her apartment.

"Umm. I don't think that's a good idea."

"Why not?"

"What's not a good idea?" Franco asked.

"Oh my god, Franco. Taste one of these cupcakes." Anna beamed with excitement.

"Lord have mercy. Those are the most gorgeous cupcakes I've ever seen. Where did you get them?"

"Taste it," she said as she unwrapped one and shoved it in his mouth.

"I think I just orgasmed." He smiled.

"Right? Aren't they fabulous?"

"I am completely jealous of the person who made these."

"See," Anna said as she turned to me. "And he's picky."

"There's no profit in that, Anna."

"Sure there is."

"Not really. Plus, did you see her? She doesn't exactly fit the business model."

"Wow. So you're saying because she's a little on the plain side, she can't sell cupcakes?" She placed her hands on her hips. "Franco, this poor woman saved up all her money with the hopes of opening a cupcake store one day and her lousy cheating bastard of a husband left her for another woman and ran off with the cash."

"That poor thing. My gosh, I don't even know her and I feel sorry for her."

"Right? But Daddy Bucks here seems to think she can't make it in the cupcake business because she's a little plain."

"I did not say that, Anna. Stop putting words in my mouth."

"You most certainly did, Mr. Carter!"

"All I'm saying is Carter Capital is not investing in a cupcake business. So drop it."

"Uh oh," Franco spoke.

"Did you just tell me to drop it?" She got in my face.

"Yes. The answer is no! I'm the business owner and I make the decision on whom to invest my money in," I sternly spoke.

"Is that so?"

"It most definitely is!"

"Well, guess what? I'm the owner of my life and I decide whom I want to spend the weekend with, and it isn't going to be you!"

"Oh come on, Anna. You're acting like a child. You don't get a say in what I invest in. You're my personal assistant, not my business partner."

"I'm going to go upstairs," Franco said as he bit down on his bottom lip.

"Did you just call me a child?"

"I said you were acting like a child. All because I don't agree with you about the cupcakes. It's like we're having a one-sided conversation and you always think you're right."

"I am right!" she yelled.

"No, you're not! You think because you were the COO of your father's company, you're right about everything?"

"You did not just say that!"

"Yeah, I did! I shouted. "You know what, maybe you're right about one thing."

"What's that?"

"That you're not spending the weekend with me. Enjoy your weekend alone." I headed towards the door.

"I'm not alone! I have Franco! Asshole!"

I shook my head, walked out the door, and then I heard a thump.

## CHAPTER TWENTY-FIVE

*Anna*

"UH!" I shouted as I stomped around the apartment.

"Calm down, Anna. Here, eat a cupcake," Franco said as he shoved one in my face.

"Can you believe what he said to me?"

"Well, it is his company and his money. If he doesn't want to invest in cupcakes, that's his decision."

"Since when do you side with him?" I shot him a look.

"I'm not siding with anyone. It's his company."

"Did you hear how he demeaned me? Telling me that I'm just his personal assistant."

"Sugar cakes, you *are* just his personal assistant. Sure, the two of you are in a relationship, but in all honesty, that doesn't give you the right to try and make his business decisions. You know I love you."

"Shut up, Franco."

I sat down on the couch and placed my face in my hands.

"Aw, come on, Anna Banana. The two of you just need a little space. You had a little spat and you'll make up as soon as you both cool down."

He didn't text me once the entire weekend and I didn't text him. Damn, was he stubborn. I strolled into the office with my head held high and a nervousness that settled in my belly. He wasn't in yet, so I listened to the voicemails that were left on the phone, wrote them down, and threw them in a messy pile on his desk with a smile.

"Morning," he mumbled as he walked into his office.

"Morning."

"How was your weekend?" he asked.

"It was good. How was yours?"

"Great. I got shitfaced with Christopher on Saturday and pretty much slept it off all day yesterday."

"Did you bring anyone home with you?"

He cocked his head at me and gave me a displeased look.

"Anna, I would never—"

"I know. I shouldn't have said that." I put up my hand.

"Come here." He held out his arms and I walked right into them. "I missed you."

"I missed you too. I'm sorry."

"Me too, sweetheart."

I broke our embrace and looked at him with a smile.

"What?" He smiled back.

"You called me 'sweetheart.'"

"I did. Because you are my sweetheart and I love you and I don't want to fight anymore."

"I love you too, Wes. I don't want to fight either."

His lips met mine for a brief moment and then he broke our kiss and locked his office door.

"What are you doing?" I asked.

"We need to make up properly." He smirked as he picked me up and carried me over to the couch.

"I think we need to fight a little more." I smiled as I slipped my shirt back on.

"I agree. Maybe we could fight some more tonight for a while and then make up again."

"Sounds good to me." I kissed his lips. "By the way, I left something on your desk."

"What is it?"

"You'll see when you open it. I better get back out there. I heard the phones ringing."

"Okay." He kissed me.

I inhaled a deep breath as I walked out of his office and braced myself. Within seconds, his door flew open.

"Get in here!" he spoke in anger.

I looked over at Tori, who was staring at me with a smile on her face. I walked back into his office as he shut the door.

"What the hell, Anna? You're quitting? You didn't even discuss it with me first!" he shouted.

"Okay. Calm down and stop yelling."

"Don't tell me to calm down! This is bullshit!" He threw the letter across his desk and rubbed his forehead. "Is this because of our fight?"

"It has something to do with it. But not because I don't like working for you. I do. Wes, this isn't for me and you know it. I'm not a personal assistant. I *have* personal assistants. I'm used to being a boss. I'm used to being in charge of things, not being in charge of other people's things."

"You're right. I'm sorry. It's just I like having you here in the office with me every day."

"And I like being here with you every day, but I can't spend the rest of my life being your personal assistant. I hope you can understand that."

"I do." He sighed. "Come here." He wrapped his arms around me, and I laid my head on his shoulder. "What are you going to do?"

"I'm going to run a cupcake business."

"What?!" He broke our embrace.

"I know you're in shock, but actually, you shouldn't be. I gave it a lot of thought over the weekend and I met with Francine. I ran the numbers and it's going to work. I'm going to make it work."

"And where are you getting the money to invest in this cupcake shop?"

"Have you forgotten who I am?" I arched my brow. "I have the money."

"You're serious about this?"

"Dead serious. We're calling it the Cupcake Nook."

"Cute name."

"It's going to be more than just a cupcake shop. We're going to have a coffee and tea station and cute little tables and chairs set up for people to come in and enjoy some coffee or tea with their cupcakes. We'll have wi-fi, and a small room off to the side where people can book it for tea parties and parents can hold birthday parties for their children. We're going to make it a big event."

He stood there with a smile on his face.

"You're really excited about this."

"I am. You wait and see, Mr. Carter, this is going to be a huge success."

"If you're running it, I have no doubt. Congratulations, Miss Young."

"Thank you." I kissed his lips.

## CHAPTER TWENTY-SIX

### Four Months Later

*Wes*

"Hey, buddy. I need you to sign this before I send it to our lawyers," Christopher spoke as he handed me a contract.

I picked up my pen, gave the contract a final look over, and signed on the dotted line.

"Want to go grab some lunch?"

"I'd love to, but I can't. I told Anna I'd drop by the shop. Tomorrow is the grand opening."

"Damn. Already?"

"Yeah. She's been working so hard. I just hope it goes well for her."

"You have your doubts?"

I leaned back in my chair and placed my hands behind my head.

"A little. I just don't think a shop like that will survive. She's going to take a big loss the first year."

"Wes, come on, she practically ran an international wine company. She knows what running a business involves. You don't need to protect her."

"But I want to protect her. I can't help it. I was walking by Cartier yesterday and I saw this beautiful ring in the window that caught my eye. I'm going to ask her to marry me."

"Seriously? Already?"

"She's the one, Christopher. The only one I want to spend the rest of my life with. I love her and I want her to be my wife."

"Wow. Congratulations." He grinned.

"Thanks. But don't congratulate me yet. She might not say yes."

"Or she might say yes and then ditch you at the altar." He laughed. "Just kidding." He put his hands up.

I grabbed my suitcoat from the back of the chair and put it on before walking out of my office and heading over to the Cupcake Nook. I walked through the door and smiled as I saw Anna standing there yelling at a contractor about something. She handed him a check and he walked away in a huff.

"What was that all about?" I asked as I wrapped my arms around her.

"He tried to rip me off and thought he could get away with it. He tried to charge me for material that wasn't even used in the store. Shady motherfucker."

I chuckled. "Nothing gets past you, does it?"

"No. Not when it's my money. I'm happy you're here. What do you think?"

"I think it's amazing. You did a great job, sweetheart. Where's Francine?"

"Right over there. Francine, come say hi to Wes."

I stared at the woman walking towards me in disbelief that it was actually Francine.

"Hi, Mr. Carter. Welcome to the Cupcake Nook." She smiled.

"Hello, Francine. The place looks great."

"Thanks. Anna and I worked really hard."

"I know you did."

"Excuse me. I'm going to go check on the cupcakes that are in the oven."

I gave her a friendly nod and then looked at Anna.

"That is not the same woman I met four months ago."

"Pretty spectacular, right? I told you I was helping her make herself over."

"She looks like a completely different woman and she seems more confident."

"That's because I taught her how to be a confident woman. Her ex-husband really shattered her self-confidence. She feels really good about her makeover, which gives her more confidence in herself."

"You did, good, sweetheart." I kissed her lips. "I need to get back to the office. I'll see you later. I love you."

"I love you too." She smiled.

After leaving the shop, I went over to Cartier and paid a visit to my friend, Marcus.

"Wes, welcome. It's always a pleasure to see you. How are your parents?"

"Good day, Marcus. The parents are good. Still traveling the world and enjoying the retired life."

"Ah. Good for them. What brings you in today?"

"I would like to take a look at a ring I saw in the window."

"Very nice. Which one?"

We walked over to the window and I pointed to the one on the pedestal that sat front and center.

"Excellent taste, Wes. Does this mean what I think it does?"

A bright smile crossed my lips. "Yes, Marcus."

"How exciting. Let's go have a seat and you can take a better look at it. This is one of our finest platinum rings with a four-carat cushion-cut high-quality flawless diamond. As you can see, the ring is set with all these brilliant pave diamonds going down each side. We just got this in a few days ago. It's part of our new exclusive collection. This is the only one made."

I held the ring up and looked at the diamonds through an eyepiece. It was truly flawless. I knew in my heart this was the ring for Anna.

"This is the one, Marcus. How much?"

"Because it's a limited ring, it's priced at a hundred thousand dollars."

"I'll take it." I grinned.

I walked out of Cartier with the ring box in my pocket. Now that I had it, I needed to find the perfect time and place to propose to her.

# CHAPTER TWENTY-SEVEN
## One Month Later

*Anna* The Cupcake Nook was a tremendous success. So much so that we needed to hire another baker and sales associate just to keep up with the demand. Francine was over the moon that everyone loved her cupcakes, just like I knew they would. If things kept going at this rate, we'd be in for a nice profit our first year.

I was back in the office going over some numbers when I heard a sweet man's voice from behind.

"Hello, gorgeous."

A smile crossed my lips as I turned around in my chair and saw Wes leaning against the doorway with his hands tucked tightly in his pants pockets.

"Hello, handsome. What are you doing here in the middle of the afternoon?"

"I wanted to surprise you. Plus, it's Tori's birthday, so I thought I'd get some cupcakes for the office."

"That's sweet of you." I made a face at him.

"I know she's not your biggest fan, but she has worked for me for a long time."

I got up from my chair and kissed his lips.

"Maybe you should fire her." I grinned.

"Maybe you should be nice."

"Whatever." I rolled my eyes. "Come on, tell me which cupcakes you want."

We walked out to the cases and Wes picked out some cupcakes for the office.

"I have a surprise for you," he spoke.

"I love surprises. What is it?"

"You'll have to wait until tonight."

"Is it something kinky?" I grinned as I leaned over the counter.

"It could be." He winked before kissing the tip of my nose. "I'll see you later."

After he walked out of the shop, Francine walked over to me.

"He's so dreamy. I wish I had one of him."

"He is, isn't he?" The corners of my mouth curved upwards as I glanced over at her. "Your dreamy guy is out there for you. You just haven't met him yet."

I stepped off the elevator and into the foyer of the penthouse. Kicking off my shoes, I walked to the kitchen, where I found Wes opening a bottle of wine. After setting the bag of Chinese food down on the island, I reached up and kissed his lips.

"Hi." I smiled.

"Hi. How was the rest of your day after I left?"

"It was busy but good."

He poured the wine into our glasses while I reached up and grabbed a couple plates down from the cabinet. I took them over to the table with the bag of food and we each took our seats and began to eat while I waited for the surprise he had for me.

"Well?" I said.

"What?"

"What's my surprise? I've been dying ever since you told me."

"I need to go to Paris for a meeting and you're coming with me." He smiled.

"Wes, that sounds wonderful, but I can't." I pouted.

"What do you mean you can't? Yes, you can, and you are."

"I can't leave the shop. Not now."

He took in a deep breath and set down his fork.

"Anna, you can leave the shop. It's only for a week. The shop will still be there when you get back."

"But it's only been open a month. I can't just walk away."

"You're not walking away, sweetheart. You're taking a much-needed vacation. You have worked your ass off in getting that shop up and ready, not to mention the countless nights we didn't see each other during the whole process. I want to take you away for some fun and relaxation and spend time alone with you. Please let me do that!" he sternly spoke as he pounded his fist on the table.

I sat there and stared at him in disbelief. His anger was turning me on.

"Okay. When do we leave?"

"We leave in a week. I already rented the private jet."

"It'll be good to see Paris again. I love it there." I smiled as I reached over and placed my hand on top of his.

～

We climbed into the car that was waiting for us at the airport when we arrived in Paris. Wes told me we were staying at the Shangri-La Hotel, but the car pulled up to the Peninsula.

"I thought we were staying at the Shangri-La," I said.

"Oops. Did I say that? My bad." He smirked.

We climbed out of the car and headed into the lobby.

"Ah, Mr. Carter, nice to see you again. Miss Young, welcome."

"You remember me?" I asked.

"Of course. How could I forget the beautiful American woman who made a fuss because the Rooftop Garden suite was already booked? The key to your suite, Mr. Carter. As always, enjoy your stay."

"Thank you."

"What suite did you get us?" I asked as we stepped into the elevator.

He glanced over at me with a smile on his face but didn't answer my question.

"You got us the Rooftop Garden suite, didn't you?"

"I did." He grinned.

"Shut up!" I playfully slapped his arm and he chuckled.

He opened the door to the suite, and the minute I walked inside, a surreal feeling washed over me as the memory of the first night we met flooded my mind.

"What's wrong?" he asked.

"Nothing. Nothing is wrong. It's just the last time we were here together, we were strangers, sharing a beautiful night and expecting never to see each other again."

He grabbed hold of my hand and led me to the living area.

"I know. That's why I wanted to stay here, in this very room, again, with you."

"I love you, Wes Carter," I softly spoke as I wrapped my arms around his neck.

"And I love you, Anna Young." His lips gently touched mine. "We need to change. I booked us a couple's massage and we need to be down in the spa in about fifteen minutes."

"Oh my god!" I spoke with excitement as I threw my head back. "That sounds wonderful."

"I knew you'd love it. So we better get moving." He slapped my ass.

# CHAPTER TWENTY-EIGHT

*Wes*

After the long flight, a couple's massage was just what we needed. It was what I needed to try and calm the nerves that were flaring up inside me. Tonight was the night. The night I'd propose to Anna and ask her to be my wife. What if she said no? Would she? I didn't think she would, but with her, you never knew. If she said no, it wouldn't be because she didn't love me. I knew she did. It would be because she wasn't ready. It wasn't all that long ago that she planned a wedding and ran from it as fast as she could. She was also still in the midst of putting everything that happened back in California behind her. I believed that was one of the reasons why she took on Francine's business, to keep herself busy to drown out the hurt she'd felt from the betrayal of her family. She hadn't spoken to her father since that day. Not because he hadn't tried to reach out to her, but because Anna said she could never forgive him. Both Nina and Matthew were indicted on embezzlement charges and received prison time.

"That was amazing." She smiled as she hooked her arm in mine and we went back up to the suite. "I'm starving. Can we go somewhere for dinner?" she asked.

"Of course." I kissed the side of her head with a smile.

We stepped into the suite and Anna and I went into the bedroom. Hanging on the closet door was the dress I ordered for her to wear tonight along with the tuxedo I ordered.

"What are these?" she asked. "They weren't here earlier."

"I had them delivered while we were down at the spa."

I took the white garment bag from the door, unzipped it, and revealed the long strapless black dress.

"This is for you to wear tonight for dinner."

"Wes, it's beautiful. Are we going somewhere super fancy?"

"Yeah." I grinned. "We are."

"How exciting! What's in this bag?" she asked.

"That's my tuxedo. We better start getting ready. I've been looking forward to seeing you in that dress since I bought it."

"Thank you. I can't wait to put it on." A bright smile crossed her face as she pressed her lips against mine.

I was standing in the living area, looking out the large window with my hands tucked into my pants pockets, when I heard Anna's voice.

"Well?" she spoke.

I turned around and gasped when I saw her standing there in her dress with her hair swept up in a beautiful updo.

"You look gorgeous." I smiled as I walked over to her.

"And you look handsome." She straightened my bowtie.

"I want to show you something?" I held out my hand.

She placed her hand in mine and I led her up the stairs and to the rooftop, where I had an elegant table with rose petals and candles lit.

"Wes, this is beautiful. You did all this?"

"I did. I wanted our first night here to be as special as possible. It's a beautiful night and I couldn't think of anything more perfect than a romantic dinner up on the rooftop overlooking Paris."

"You are truly a dream come true." She smiled as she kissed me.

I pulled out her chair and she took a seat. Pulling out my phone, I sent a message to the chef that we were ready for dinner. Within moments, a waiter came up and filled our glasses with champagne and brought an appetizer to start.

"This is truly amazing, Wes. Look at that view."

"As beautiful as it is, I'd rather look at you."

I nervously placed my hand in my pocket, pulled out the ring box, and held it under the table while I took in a deep breath.

"Anna, I love you."

"I love you too." She smiled.

"It wasn't that long ago that we were here, in this room together, sharing a beautiful night of passion. I never told you this, but I considered staying because there was something about you that pulled me in. The more I thought about it, I couldn't, because I knew once we had our time here, I'd never see you again and it would be too hard. Then you showed up at my office, and once again, you were in my life. I can't even explain to you the happiness that consumed me when I saw you standing in the doorway of my conference room."

"I felt the same way," she softly spoke as tears infiltrated her eyes.

I got up from my seat, walked over to her chair, and got down on one knee while I opened the lid of the box and held it up in front of her. Immediately, she placed her hand over her mouth.

"I love you, Anna Young, and I want to spend the rest of my life with you. Will you marry me and do me the honor of becoming my wife?"

She placed her hand on my cheek as a tear fell from her eye.

"Yes. Yes. Yes. I will marry you, Wes Carter. I can't believe this."

I removed the ring from the box, took her left hand, and slid it on her finger.

"It's a perfect fit." She smiled as she stared at it. "Wes, it's stunning."

"You're stunning, Anna."

I helped her up from her chair and wrapped my arms around her waist while hers wrapped around my neck. We stared into each other's eyes before our lips met with desire. My heart filled with happiness that she said yes, but I had another worry.

## CHAPTER TWENTY-NINE

*Anna*

His lips grazed my neck as he held my arms above my head and moved in and out of me at a steady pace. I gasped for air with each long stroke as my body took him in, stimulating me beyond glory. I let out a moan as my body tightened and an orgasm rushed through me. His breath became heavier as he picked up the pace and came with me.

He hovered over me with a smile upon his lips as little beads of sweat covered his forehead.

"I don't think I can move." He chuckled.

"Me either." I smiled.

He gathered the energy to roll off me and I snuggled my body against his, resting my head on his chest, staring at the beautiful ring that sat upon my finger.

"Isn't it ironic that the last time we lay in this bed together, we were complete strangers, and now we're lying in this bed for the second time in our lives and we're engaged. Who would have thought that our one night in Paris would have led to this?"

"I agree." His grip around me tightened.

"Oh my god," she spoke as she sat up and looked at me.

"What is it?"

"This is the reason why you were so mad at me when I told you that I couldn't come to Paris with you."

"I wondered how long it was going to take you to figure that out." He smiled as he brought his finger up and softly traced my lips.

"Ugh, and to think I almost ruined it. I'm sorry, Wes."

"You're here and that's all that matters, sweetheart."

"You don't have a meeting tomorrow, do you?"

"No." He grinned. "It was an excuse to get you here."

"I have to Facetime Franco," I excitedly spoke as I reached over and grabbed my phone from the nightstand.

"Here, put on your robe first."

I took the robe he handed me and slipped it on. I brought up Franco's number and Facetimed him.

"Hello, my love. Oh. I see you're already christening the hotel room." He smiled.

"We are." I grinned. "Say hi to Wes." I turned the phone to him.

"Hello, Wes." Franco waved.

"Hey, Franco."

"Guess what?" I beamed with excitement.

"What?"

I held my hand with my ring on it up to the phone.

"Wes asked me to marry him!" I squealed.

"AH! I'm so happy for you! Holy shit, look at that ring. It's gorgeous, Anna."

"Thank you. Okay. I have to go now. I need to get back to my fiancé. I'll talk to you later. Love you."

"Love you too, baby doll."

"When we get back to New York, I want you to permanently move in with me."

"Is that a command, Mr. Carter? Or a request?"

"It's a command and I'm not taking no for an answer."

"Good. Because I love your commands." I grinned as I leaned over and kissed him.

∾

Paris was amazing and we were now back to the land of reality. With Franco's help, I moved all of my things out of his apartment and over to Wes' penthouse, which was now my new permanent home.

"I want to show you something," Franco said as he grabbed his sketchbook. "I've been working on a design for your wedding dress. Tell me what you think."

I took the sketch from his hand and studied the drawing.

"Franco, it's beautiful. Oh my god, I love it."

"Do you like the style? I wanted to do something different than your last one. This one is going to be even more spectacular."

"I love it. It's perfect." I gave him a smile.

"Good. I'm glad the two of you already set the date, so now I know what kind of timeframe I'm working with. By the way, have you told your father?"

"No." I looked away and went into the kitchen for a cup of coffee. "And I'm not. He's not a part of my life and he doesn't need to know. Which brings me to this. I would be honored if you would walk me down the aisle."

He brought his hand up to his mouth and I could see a hint of tears filling his eyes.

"I would be so honored to walk you down the aisle. You are my best friend in the whole world."

"Stop!" I waved my hands in front of my face as the tears swelled. I gave him a hug and thanked him.

# CHAPTER THIRTY

## Three Months Later

*Anna*

Happy wasn't a word that could describe how I felt inside. My life was finally perfect—the kind of perfection I'd always dreamed of. Something I never thought I'd have or experience. I was sitting on the couch, going over some orders for the shop, when I heard the elevator ding and Wes stepped out.

"Hey, sweetheart." He smiled as he walked over to me and kissed my lips.

"Hi. How was your day?"

"Exhausting. If anything could go wrong, it did."

He walked over to the bar and poured himself a scotch.

"Do you want one?" he asked.

"No. I'm good." I smiled.

He downed his drink and poured another one.

"Serena brought her baby in the office today for the first time. She's due back from her maternity leave next week. Her son is so cute and tiny. I held him."

"You did?"

"Yeah. For quite a while. He seemed to like me."

"That's because you're extremely likeable, Mr. Carter." I grinned.

"You know, I got to thinking about how we have never talked about children. How many kids do you want?"

I looked at him and gulped. There was a reason this subject never came up.

"Wes, I don't ever want children."

"What?" he asked as he walked over to me. "What do you mean?"

"I never have, and to be honest, I don't plan on having any."

"Anna, I don't understand."

"I assumed you never wanted them either since we never talked about it."

"I love kids, and yes, I want them. I guess we never talked about it because we were so wrapped up in everything else. You're seriously going to sit there and tell me that you don't want to have children with me?"

"You act like you're taking this personally, Wes. I just don't want children period."

"Why? Because of your mother?" His eye narrowed at me.

"Don't. Don't do this." I shook my head as I got up from the couch. "Don't bring her into this."

"I am doing this." His voice grew louder. "If it's because of her, maybe need to get some therapy."

"Excuse me? You're standing there telling me that I need therapy because I don't want kids?"

"Who the hell doesn't want kids, Anna?" he yelled as he held out his arms.

"There are lots of people in this world that don't want kids."

"That's just insane." He finished off his scotch and walked back to the bar.

"Oh. So now I'm insane because I don't want kids. Do you hear yourself?" I shouted.

"We're having kids, Anna."

"Is that so?" I stood there with my hands on my hips. "I hate to tell you this, Wes, but it's my body, and if I don't want kids, I'm not having any."

"Man, I wish we would have discussed this before—"

"Before what, Wes?" I asked in a harsh tone.

"Nothing. Listen, Anna, let's discuss this like mature adults. I want nothing more than to have a baby with you someday. It doesn't have to be now or in a year," he calmly spoke. "I can wait until you're ready."

"I'll never be ready. I don't want children. Not now, not ever, and I'm not going to stand here and tell you okay and give you false hope, and then in a couple of years, we're standing in this exact spot having the same argument. I don't want children. Period."

He stood a few feet away from me with anger in his eyes. An anger I'd never seen before from him.

"Then why are we doing this?" he asked.

"What? Getting married? Because we love each other. Have you forgotten that? You're going to let something like me not wanting children ruin us?"

"It's like I don't even know you, Anna. You won't even consider it a possibility?"

"No, because I'm not going to lie to you. I'm being honest, Wes. I'm being real and raw here."

"Relationships are based on compromise. I've compromised a lot with you on all sorts of things and now you won't even extend me the courtesy of considering having a family?"

"No. I won't. There's nothing to consider. I don't want kids."

"I'm sorry you feel that way. Maybe this isn't going to work out after all," he somberly spoke as he held out his hand.

I couldn't believe this was happening as my body shook from head to toe and my heart was pounding out of my chest. I removed the ring from my finger and placed it in his hand.

"Don't do this, Wes," I spoke as numerous tears fell down my face.

"I'm sorry, Anna. You and I want two totally different things, and if this is something we can't see eye to eye on, then there's no point in moving forward." His eyes swelled with tears. "I'm leaving. I'll give you a couple of hours to gather your things and move out. If you need more time than that, let me know."

He walked away and pushed the button to the elevator. I ran to him and grabbed his arm.

"Don't," I cried. "Please."

He jerked his arm out of my grip and stepped into the elevator.

The doors shut and I fell to my knees and pounded on them as I screamed his name. I gathered myself from the floor, shaking and crying like my life had just been ripped away from me. I walked up the stairs, grabbed my suitcase from the closet, and threw some of my clothes into it. I went into the bathroom, gathered my makeup and toiletries, and threw them in a duffle bag. Grabbing my phone, I texted Franco.

*"Are you home?"*

*"I just walked in. Why?"*

*"I need to talk to you. I'm on my way over."*

*"Okay. I'll be here. Everything okay?"*

I didn't respond and tossed my phone in my purse. I grabbed the duffle bag and my suitcase and headed out of the penthouse. I arrived at Franco's apartment and lightly knocked on the door. I didn't feel like digging out my key.

"Why didn't you—Anna, what happened?" he asked as he looked down and saw my suitcase.

I broke down and my bottom lip started to quiver.

"Wes left me."

"What? Get in here."

He pulled me into his apartment and then grabbed my suitcase. Placing his hands on my shoulders, he led me over to the couch.

"What happened? Why would he leave you?"

"He wants kids and I don't. We got into a huge fight about it and he said if I didn't want them, then there was no use in moving forward." I cried on his shoulder.

"Shit. It's okay." He held me. "Everything is going to be okay."

# CHAPTER THIRTY-ONE

*Wes*

I took a cab to the heart of Hell's Kitchen and entered a bar called Pocket Bar. After planting myself on a stool, the bartender walked over to me.

"What can I get you, man?"

"Scotch on the rocks and keep them coming."

"Sure thing," he said as he tapped his knuckles on the counter.

I pulled out my phone and dialed Christopher.

"Hey, Wes."

"Can you meet me in Hell's Kitchen at the Pocket Bar? I need to talk to you."

"Sure. Is everything okay?"

"No. It's not. I'll see you soon."

The bartender set my drink in front of me and I downed it like it was water. He poured me another and I sat there, holding it between my hands, thinking about Anna and everything that was said and happened.

"Hey," Christopher said as he walked up from behind and placed his hand on my shoulder. He took a seat next to me and ordered a scotch. "What's going on?"

"Anna doesn't want kids."

"Why?"

"Because of her mother and what happened to her, even though she won't admit it."

"Gee, Wes, I'm sorry. The two of you never discussed kids before?"

"No, and I'm glad I brought it up today. Could you imagine if I married her and then found out."

"Bro, what do you mean 'if?'"

"I broke up with her, took the ring back, and told her to move out."

"You're kidding me."

"No. I'm not." I glanced over at him as I brought my glass up to my lips. "I thought I knew her. I guess I didn't."

"Maybe she'll change her mind. She loves you and you love her. You can't let something like this tear you apart."

"She won't change her mind. Bartender." I held up my glass. "She was very adamant about it."

"Wes, you love her more than life."

"I know and I also love children. You knew how happy I was when Alexa told me she was pregnant. Even though I wasn't in love with her, I was ecstatic that I was going to be a father. Then you saw what it did to me when I found out she lied. I've always wanted a family, and when I met Anna and fell in love with her, I thought she loved me enough to want to have one with me."

"She does love you. The two of you can work this out. Come on, bro." He hooked his arm around me. "Don't let this destroy what the two of you have. I'm sorry that I have to say this, but there's more to life than wanting kids. You have to step outside the box and look at the bigger picture."

"I have looked at the bigger picture, and it consisted of me and Anna at home with small children running around us. That was my bigger picture, Christopher, and without that, I don't see how the two of us together can work. If we were together, in the back of my mind, I'd always resent her for not wanting to start a family, and she'd always resent me for wanting one."

I threw back the last of my scotch and Christopher helped me home.

## CHAPTER THIRTY-TWO

*Anna*
A couple of days had passed, and I didn't get out of bed once. I couldn't. I didn't have the strength after all the crying I'd done. All of this because he wanted kids and I didn't. Franco took care of me the best he could, and I willingly let him.

"Anna, you need to get out of this bed. In all my years of knowing you, I have never seen you like this. You're stronger than this, girl. I'm worried about you, and if you don't get up, I'm going to have you committed to a psych hospital."

I pushed the covers back that were covering my head and looked at him.

"That's a good idea. I think I belong there."

A smile crossed his lips. "There's my girl."

"Franco, I can't get up. I seriously don't even want to deal with life."

"Anna, you haven't showered in days, and what about the shop?"

"Francine thinks I have the flu."

"Listen, girl. I love you to pieces but get your sorry ass out of bed right now."

He set a piece of paper down on the nightstand.

"I'm giving you tough love because I love you and I'm worried. I made an appointment for you to see a therapist. His name is Dr. Stark and he's supposedly the best in Manhattan. I got his name and number from a friend of mine. Your appointment is for three o'clock. Luckily, they had a cancellation today. You better go, Anna. I have to run. I have a meeting with a client." He kissed my forehead and walked out of the room.

I let out a huff and pulled the covers back over my head. A few moments later, I threw them back and sat up. Looking over at the nightstand, I picked up the piece of paper and looked at it. Damn him. I climbed out of bed and hopped into the shower, got myself together, and went downstairs. I couldn't believe Wes hadn't bothered to call or text me. It was obvious he didn't care. I grabbed my purse and headed out the door to Dr. Stark's office.

∽

I signed in and took a seat in the waiting room. I didn't need this, and I didn't belong here. I changed my mind. I was out. Just as I got up from my seat to walk out the door, a tall and handsome older man with long hair, casual clothes, and beads around his neck stepped into the waiting area and called my name.

"Anna?" He smiled. "You're not trying to escape, are you?"

"Caught me." I nervously laughed.

"I'm Dr. Stark. I know it's hard being here, especially if you've never been to a therapist's office before. It can be intimidating. Come with me to my space and give me a chance. If you don't like our conversation, then you won't ever have to come back. Deal?"

I liked him. He seemed nice and genuine and from another decade. There was something about his voice that made me feel comfortable.

"Deal." I smiled.

"I ask when we get to my office, you remove your shoes," he said.

*Okay. This guy is weird.*

I followed him into his office and was taken aback by the décor. I removed my shoes and set them on the shoe rack by the door. I looked around at the orange-painted walls with different types of tapestries that hung on them, all in bold and beautiful colors and designs. Beads hung down off the to the side, separating this room from another. Large round pillow chairs that sat on the ground in different colors graced the space as well as a teal-colored futon with multi-print pillows that lined the wall.

"May I offer you some coffee or water?" he asked.

"Coffee would be great. Umm. Your office is really cool."

"Thanks. But I don't consider it an office. It's a gathering space where people can be comfortable and relax."

"Let me guess, you never got out of the seventies. Did you?" I smirked.

"Nope." He smiled as he handed me my coffee. "Sit anywhere you want. Couch, chair, floor. Feel free to lie on the floor if you want. Stretch out, cross your legs. The most important thing is that you're comfortable and you don't feel like you're in therapy."

I took a seat on the teal-colored couch and brought my legs up to my chest as I sipped my coffee. This was kind of cool and I felt more relaxed than I had in days. He sat Indian-style on one of the big fluffy pillow chairs across from me and I found myself talking non-stop when he asked why I was there.

"Do you hate children?" he asked me.

"No. Of course not. I like children."

"But you don't want any of your own because you're afraid you'll fuck them up like your parents did you, right?"

*Okay. Wow. This guy is raw.*

"I don't consider myself fucked-up, Dr. Stark. I am an independent woman who knows what she wants."

"And kids are what you don't want."

"Right. I don't want children."

"Because you're afraid you'll fuck them up like your parents did you."

"Yes," I involuntarily blurted out." *Damn it.*

He looked at me with a smile and nodded his head.

"Congratulations, Anna. You just took the first step in healing yourself."

We talked some more, and when the timer went off, I didn't want to leave. I felt like we were making some sort of progress.

"Do you think you want to come back and chat again?" he asked.

"Yes, Dr. Stark. I do. I actually want to come every day if possible."

"Every day?" he asked with surprise.

"Yes. We have a lot of ground to cover. I don't care what it costs because I can afford it. So pencil me in for the rest of the week. And if you can't get me in, then make it after hours and I will pay double your fee."

"Okay. Cindy will set up the appointments for you." He smiled.

I walked out of his space and hailed a cab back to the apartment. When I walked in, Franco was in the kitchen cooking.

"How did it go?" he asked without turning around.

"It was fabulous. I love Dr. Stark. He is so cool, and his space is like I was transported to the 70's."

He turned around and looked at me with a shocked expression on his face.

"You, Anna Young, liked therapy?"

"It's not therapy. It's chatting." I smiled.

He walked over to me and placed his hands on each side of my face and forcefully planted a kiss on my lips.

"It is so good to hear you say that and to see you smile again."

"I have an appointment with him every day this week. I told him we have a lot of ground to cover. Thanks, Franco."

"You're welcome, sweet cheeks."

# CHAPTER THIRTY-THREE

## Wes

Three weeks had passed, and I hadn't seen or heard from Anna. I'd been a bear to anyone who crossed my path. My bed at night was lonely and even lonelier in the mornings. I couldn't bear to go home after the office anymore because everything there reminded me of her. The home I once loved was now the place I dreaded the most.

It was the middle of the afternoon and I was walking down West 84th Street when I saw Anna turn the corner. I quickly stepped into a store and watched her pass by. She looked beautiful, but the spark in her eye wasn't there. I stepped out of the store and followed her, mixing in with the street crowd so she wouldn't notice me. She went inside a building, and when I reached it, I looked at the name that was engraved on a brass plate that hung on the brick wall to the left of the door, *Dr. Nathan Stark, PsyD.* A psychologist? She was seeing a psychologist?

Later that night, as I was sitting in my usual spot at the Post Bar, the door opened. When I turned around to see what all the noise was, I noticed a group of people filtered inside. My heart started racing when I saw Anna amongst those people. I turned around, desperately trying to remain calm as I threw back my drink and asked the bartender for another one.

"Wes?" I heard her soft voice from behind.

*Shit.*

I turned around as she stood there, and our eyes locked on to each other's.

"Anna. What are you doing here?"

"It's Lars' birthday. Are you here alone?"

"Yeah. I am."

"Why?"

"Why not?" I spoke deadpan as I turned around. "I'm sorry. I just didn't expect to see you."

"I didn't expect to see you either. How are you?"

"As good as can be expected, I guess. How are you?"

"The same as you."

"You better get back to your friends," I said as I finished off my drink, threw some cash on the counter, and got up from my seat.

"Yeah. I guess I better. It was good to see you."

"Yeah." I nodded and walked out the door.

Instead of hailing a cab right away, I started walking down the street. I needed the air. It had seemed she moved on. She was out with her friends having fun while I sat in a bar alone. My choice, I know, but I couldn't bring myself to have any type of fun since our breakup.

"Wes!" I heard her shout.

I stopped dead center in the middle of the sidewalk while people pushed their way around me. I didn't turn around. I couldn't.

"You asked me how I was, and I lied to you," she said from behind. "I'm not as good as could be expected. In fact, I'm not good at all. I hate that this happened with us. I cry myself to sleep every night and wish you were lying next to me. I check my phone a hundred times a day wishing and hoping that it would ring and you'd be on the other end. I miss you, Wes."

I slowly turned around and looked at the sadness in her eyes, the same sadness I had in mine. I wanted to reach out and grab her and tell her that everything was going to be okay, but I wasn't sure if it ever would be again.

"I miss you too, Anna."

"Can we go somewhere and talk?" she asked.

"Don't you have a party to join?"

"They can party without me. I didn't even feel like coming, but Franco dragged me out of the apartment."

"I'm not sure there's anything to talk about. We're just going to rehash the same old shit and end up in another argument."

"Is that how you really feel?" she asked.

"It doesn't matter how I feel. It's the truth. I want a family with you and you don't. What's left to say?"

"I have a lot to say, and so do you. Even if you don't want to admit it. I have fears that I should have expressed to you, but instead, I shut down and stood my ground. I shouldn't have been so quick to react the way I did."

"You're right, I do have a lot to say, but I don't want to hurt you any more than you're already hurting."

"It's okay. I can take it. I know it's been three weeks and it's been the longest three weeks of my life. But I've been in therapy every day and Dr. Stark has really helped me to see things in a different light."

"Every day?" I asked.

"Yes. I told him we had a lot of ground to cover."

I couldn't help but let out a chuckle.

"Where do you want to talk?" I asked.

"Central Park would be a good place."

"Central Park it is."

We took a cab over to the entrance of Central Park where Cherry Hill was. It was quiet there and a beautiful night to sit by the lake and talk. Before we made it there, Anna had the cab driver stop at her apartment so she could grab a blanket for us to sit on. I couldn't help but smile when she suggested it. Once we arrived, we spread out the blanket and we both sat down.

"I have a mechanism inside me that shuts down when someone tells me what they want from me. It's a fear mechanism because of how I was raised. If something scares me enough, I shut down instantly, and I close myself off. When you brought up the subject of children, the only thing I could see was me not being able to love and nurture that child like my mother couldn't me. It wasn't a fear I was projecting on myself; it was out of fear for the child. That's why I never wanted kids. Because I was so afraid of fucking them up and putting them through what I went through. I'm literally scared to be a mom, and over the years, I created this story in my mind and I made myself believe that I would be a horrible mother like mine was. Don't get me wrong, Wes, I love kids. I really do. I'm just afraid for them and you."

"Me? Why me?"

"Because I saw how it hurt my father and I saw how after time, he resented me for it, and it tore my parents apart."

"You're not your mother, Anna, and I'm not your father. I understand your fear, I really do. When Alexa told me that she was pregnant, I was over the moon with happiness. Even though I didn't love her, I was going to be a father. Then, when I found out that there was never a baby, it destroyed me. I spent years hiding myself from women because I couldn't trust them. Then I met you and you changed all that for me. All I could see was us having a family together. Then when you said you didn't ever want to have kids, like you, I shut down and walked away thinking it would be easier instead of standing there while you broke my heart. But it hasn't been easy at all. I've been a total mess these past three weeks. I wanted to reach out to you, but I didn't want to bear any more pain. For fuck sakes, this isn't worth it. Being without you is not worth it. Any of it. If you don't want kids, I can live with that, Anna. Because all I want is to spend the rest of my life with you."

"No, you can't, Wes. Just like I can't live with not having a family with you."

"What? What are you saying?"

"I'm saying that I can't, and I won't let my fear stop me from living my best life. My best life is being with you, marrying you and starting a family. I let my parents and their issues define me and I'm not letting them do that anymore. They may have created me and given birth to me, but they aren't me and I'm not them. And when we do have children one day and some signs appear that need addressing, I'll get the help I need right away."

"I've missed you so much," I spoke as I placed my hands on each side of her face.

"I missed you too."

I leaned in and brushed my lips against hers. Within seconds, our kiss deepened, and I never wanted to let her go. We both fell back on the blanket and laughed. We were making out in Central Park like a couple of teenagers. I broke our kiss and stared into her eyes as the light of the moon glistened on the lake.

"Can I you take you home? Back to our home?"

"Yes." She smiled. "I want to come home."

## CHAPTER THIRTY-FOUR

### Six Months Later

*Wes*

I paced back and forth while I tried to calm my nerves. Today was our wedding day and I couldn't help but have this feeling inside me. I needed to talk to Franco, so I found Francine and told her to get him for me and meet me outside the church.

"Wes, you wanted to see me?"

"Franco, how is she?"

"She's simply gorgeous." He grinned. "You'll get to see for yourself in a bit."

"I know she's gorgeous. That's not what I meant. I mean, how is she feeling?"

"She's feeling fine." His eye narrowed at me.

"Fine as in she's sure about this?"

"I'm confused, Wes. What is going on here?"

"I need you to do me one favor and one favor only. Make. Sure. She. Gets. Down. That. Aisle."

"Oh." He chuckled. "That's what you're worried about. Please, Wes, she loves you to death. She's walking down that aisle. Trust me."

"Okay." I nervously nodded.

"Now go back inside the church and take your place. We'll see you in a few." He winked.

∽

*Anna*

"Is everything okay? Francine said Wes wanted to see you. Is he having second thoughts?" I asked in a panicked tone.

"Darling, relax. I honestly don't know what is wrong with you two. Now turn and look at yourself one last time before you become Mrs. Westin Carter. We need to make sure everything is perfect."

I stood in front of the full-length mirror while Franco placed the veil he made me on my head.

"I will say, I do believe I outdid myself even more this time around."

"You did, Franco. Thank you for everything."

"You're welcome, love. Are you ready to become Mrs. Westin Carter?" He held out his arm.

"I am." I grinned as I hooked my arm around his.

As soon as the music began to play, Franco and I started to slowly walk down the long aisle. I gulped as I stared at my future husband, who stood there with a smile on his face. Instantly, I stopped.

"Anna, what are you doing?" Franco asked in a whisper.

"I'm sorry, Franco," I spoke as I kissed his cheek, handed him my bouquet and kicked off my shoes.

Picking up my dress, I ran down the aisle with a smile on my face and right into the arms of my handsome husband-to-be. He laughed as he picked me up and swung me around.

"I love you." I smiled.

"I love you too, sweetheart."

"Are you ready to marry me?" I asked.

"I've never been more ready for anything in my life. Let's do this."

"Brilliant, darling. This is why I love you," Franco whispered as he handed me my shoes and bouquet.

Our ceremony was beautiful, and after taking several wedding pictures, we headed to our reception which was held at the Mandarin Oriental. We partied the night away with our friends and family and then headed up to our honeymoon suite for a night neither one of us would ever forget. In the morning, we'd leave for our honeymoon. Two weeks of just us. No business, no phones, nothing. Just us, Bora Bora, and Bali.

## CHAPTER THIRTY-FIVE
### Six Months Later

*Anna*

"I'll see you tomorrow, Francine," I said as I grabbed my purse and walked out of the shop.

As I walked down the street to the drugstore, my belly started to flutter with nerves as I entered through the door and looked up at the signs that hung above each aisle. Found it. Aisle four. I stood in front of the shelf and looked at the vast amounts of pregnancy tests that were staring back at me. I was confused. It shouldn't be this hard. My god, why were there so many different ones? This was ridiculous. I carefully looked at each one: digital results, rapid results, week indicator results, colored results, word results, smart countdown results. My head was spinning, for I knew nothing about pregnancy tests. I walked up to the front of the store and grabbed a small basket. Taking it back to aisle four, I grabbed a few different ones off the shelf and threw them in the basket. Then I hit the candy aisle and grabbed a couple Hershey bars, a bag of M&M's for Wes, and a couple packs of Reese's peanut butter cups for us to share.

As soon as I stepped into the penthouse, Wes came walking from his study.

"Did you get one?" he asked as he kissed me.

"It was overwhelming, so I got a few." I opened the bag and showed him.

"Hmm. Do you really think you need that many?"

"I don't know. Why not?" I smiled. "I'll just pee on them all."

He stuck his hand in the bag and pulled out his M&M's.

"For me?"

"Of course. We're going to need to snack while we wait."

"Great idea. Shall we?" He held out his hand.

"We shall." I placed my hand in his and we walked upstairs.

I dumped the bag on the bathroom counter. Wes and I began opening the boxes, and I carefully read the directions for each one.

"They're all the same," I spoke. "So just hand them to me one by one, I'll pee on the stick and then you line them up in a row. Let your OCD shine." I smirked.

"Do you have enough pee in you to do all these?"

"I've been holding it for a long time. Trust me, I have more than enough."

I took down my pants and sat on the toilet.

"Are you ready?" he asked as he held the first stick in front of me.

"I'm ready." I took in a deep breath.

We were like an assembly line. Stick, pee, return. Stick, pee, return. Stick. Pee. Return. When I was finished, I got up, washed my hands, grabbed my Hershey bar, and Wes and I walked out of the bathroom and took a seat on the edge of the bed.

"Three minutes for each of them. So let's set the timer for five minutes because we have to give the last couple ones I did time to cook." I grinned.

"Okay. Setting the timer for five minutes," he spoke.

We sat there together. Wes shook some M&M's in his hand and popped them into his mouth while I broke off three squares of chocolate and ate them.

"Want some?" he asked as he tilted the bag towards me.

"No. Thanks. Want some Hershey's?" I asked as I tilted the candy bar to him.

"Nah. I'm good."

Five minutes was nothing, but to us, it was the longest five minutes of our lives. If I was pregnant, it wasn't planned. We talked about waiting a year or two after we were married to start trying. But we didn't care. We were happy and prayed that the results were positive. The timer went off on his phone, and after he shut it off, he took hold of my hand and brought it up to his lips.

"If you're not. It's okay," he softly spoke.

"I know. We still have plenty of time. It's not like it was planned or anything."

"I totally agree, sweetheart. Are you ready?"

"I am." I took in a deep breath.

As he still was holding my hand, we both got up and slowly walked to the bathroom, both of us stopping in the doorway. We stood and stared at the line of sticks from afar for a moment before walking up to the counter and viewing the results.

"They're all positive, Anna," Wes said with excitement in his voice.

"I'm pregnant!" I grinned.

"Wait, what does this one mean? It says 3+."

"That's the week indicator one. I must be three weeks or more."

We turned to each other and Wes placed his hands on each side of my face.

"We're having a baby." The corners of his mouth curved upwards.

"We're having a baby." I smiled brightly as our lips met and we shared a long passionate kiss.

"I have to tell Franco. Like, right now," I said.

"Call him up and invite him over for dinner. I have a plan on how we can tell him."

We walked out of the bathroom and I grabbed my phone and dialed his number.

"Hello, lovely."

"Hi, Franco. Wes and I want you to come over for dinner tonight if you're available."

"Dinner? How fun. You're lucky you caught me on a night that I'm not doing anything. Actually, even if I was, you know I'd cancel to spend the evening with the two of you. What time?"

"How about an hour?"

"Perfect. Tell Wes I just made a fresh cheesecake that I'll bring."

"You know, Franco. I've been thinking about this lately. You started making those cheesecakes for me and now you're making them for Wes?"

"I'm sensing some juju jealousy coming from you, Anna Banana."

"Just bring the cheesecake and get your ass over here. I'm hungry."

"Did I hear he made me a cheesecake?" Wes grinned.

"Yes. He made you a cheesecake." I rolled my eyes.

He wrapped his arm around me and we fell onto the bed.

"We have some time to celebrate privately." He grinned.

"Then let's celebrate."

After we celebrated the news of my pregnancy with amazing sex, Wes and I got dressed and went down to the kitchen.

"There's no time to cook," I said. "We better just order in something."

"Thai?" he asked.

"Sounds good. You already what Franco likes."

"I'll go place the order now."

A few moments later, I heard a ding and Franco's voice as he stepped off the elevator.

"Hello, Carter fam. I've arrived, and I brought some goodies."

Wes and Franco walked into the kitchen together.

"Hello, sugar plum." Franco smiled as he kissed my cheek.

"Hi." I grinned. "I ran out of time to cook, so we're ordering Thai."

"Thai sounds fabulous."

"Thanks again for the cheesecake, Franco." Wes smiled as he held it up before putting it in the refrigerator.

"Anything for you, Mr. Carter."

I narrowed my eye at both of them.

"Oh stop." Franco patted my arm. "So when's the food going to be here? This man is famished."

"It should be here in about fifteen minutes. Can I get you a drink, Franco?" Wes asked.

"I'll take a nice glass of Chardonnay."

"Anna?" Wes asked as he winked at me.

"I'll wait until the food gets here. Franco, is there any way you can fix my pants? The zipper broke today when I was zipping them up."

"Of course. Let me look at them. Are they down here?"

"Actually, they're in the master bathroom. Can you just run up and get them while I set the table?"

"Sure thing. I'll be right back."

If there was one thing I knew about Franco, it was his scream when he was overly excited. Wes stood next to me and placed his arm around my waist as we stood there and patiently waited for it. And there it was. Wes turned to me and we both smiled. Within seconds, he came flying down the stairs and stopped in the entrance of the kitchen.

"We're having a baby!" he screamed as he jumped up and down and clapped his hands.

"YES! We're having a baby!"

"Oh my god. I can't believe it."

He walked over and wrapped his arms around both of us, pulling us into a group hug.

"I'm so happy for the both of you," he spoke.

## CHAPTER THIRTY-SIX

*Anna*

Wes went with me to my first doctor's appointment to confirm that I was indeed pregnant. Six weeks to be exact. We were both so over the moon with excitement, but there was a part of me that still harbored a fear, so I made an appointment with Dr. Stark.

"That's wonderful news, Anna. Congratulations."

"Thank you, Dr. Stark. Wes and I are so happy, but—"

"But you're nervous about what's going to happen after the pregnancy?"

"Yes."

"Anna, you're a young healthy woman and you're glowing. Worrying about it isn't going to help you or the baby. It's only going to stress you both out. Here's what I want you to start doing. I want you to take fifteen minutes every day and meditate. Clear your mind and your thoughts. I have some great meditation practices I can give you. Also, I want you to practice Kundalini yoga at least three times a week. You can take a class or hire a private instructor. I promise you that if you do those two things and you start now, you will have nothing to worry about."

"Thanks, Dr. Stark. I will definitely start both of them immediately."

*Wes*

The months went by and Anna was already six months pregnant. Her belly grew every day and she looked even more beautiful now than she did when I first laid eyes on her. When she had her ultrasound, we found out we were having a girl. To be honest, I didn't care what sex the baby was as long as it was healthy. But when I heard those words "you're having a girl," I felt a tug in my heart. We started working on the nursery. Anna suggested we decorate in a Paris theme because that was where we met, and Paris would always hold a special meaning in our lives.

I climbed into bed next to Anna, who was reading *What to Expect When You're Expecting*. I pulled the covers back that covered her, lifted up her nightshirt, and firmly placed my lips against her belly.

"Hello, baby girl. How was your day?"

"What are you doing?" Anna laughed.

"What's that?" I placed my ear against her belly. "Your mommy ate the last piece of cheesecake?"

"Oh my god, stop it!" She ran her fingers through my hair.

I let out a chuckle as I pulled her nightshirt down and reached up and kissed her lips.

"I love us." I smiled.

"I love us too."

*Anna*

I was thirty-seven weeks pregnant and more than ready to have this kid. Everything was set and now all we needed was her to come into the world. About a month ago, Franco threw us the most amazing and elegant baby shower. Wes and I were blown away at the generosity of our family and friends.

As I was climbing out of bed, I stopped and placed my hand on my belly.

"Are you okay, Anna?" Wes asked as he stepped out from the bathroom.

"Yeah. Just those damn Braxton Hicks. I'm fine."

"Maybe you should stay home and rest."

"I'm fine, Wes. I have work to do at the shop."

"Maybe you should stop working now until after the baby is born."

"Maybe you shouldn't have said such a silly thing." I narrowed my eye at him.

"Right. Go to work, Anna. Just don't work too hard." He walked over and kissed my head.

"Thank you, and I won't."

As I was in the bathroom putting my makeup on, Wes walked up behind me and planted his hands on my belly.

"I have to go." He softly kissed my neck.

"Have a good day." I reached back and placed my hand behind his head.

He turned me around, bent down, and kissed our baby goodbye.

"Now don't give your mommy any trouble today. I can tell she's tired because you were kicking her all night."

"I swear this kid is going to be a kickboxer or something. She's strong."

"She's like her mom." He smiled as he stood up and kissed me goodbye.

# CHAPTER THIRTY-SEVEN

*Anna*

I waddled into the shop and the first thing I did was take a chocolate cupcake and eat it.

"Breakfast?" Francine smiled.

"Actually, I had oatmeal before I came in. So I'm considering this a mid-morning snack."

I went into my office to look over some reports. The shop was doing phenomenal, and in our first year, we made a big profit. I knew this business would do well, and now Wes was regretting he didn't invest himself. I finished up what I had to do and decided to go see if they needed any help up front. I was standing behind the counter, when the door opened. I looked up and my eyes met with the same eyes staring back at me. I froze and my heart started racing.

"Anna?" The woman's soft voice spoke as she placed her hand over her mouth.

If I ran, I'd look like an idiot. Plus, I was thirty-seven weeks pregnant. Running wasn't possible.

"Carla," I spoke.

She was with a man I presumed was her husband. Panic started to soar through me, but I remembered my breathing and quickly tried to calm myself down. Her husband grasped her shoulders when he heard my name. God, what I wouldn't give for Wes to be here.

"How are you?" she cautiously asked as she approached the counter.

"I'm great. I'm pregnant." I placed my hands on my belly.

"I can see that." She smiled. "You look like you're due very soon."

"In about two and a half weeks. What are you doing here in New York?" I asked.

"We're looking at places to live. We may move here."

*Shit. Shit. Shit.*

"I didn't know you lived here. Aren't you working for your father anymore?"

"No. Things weren't working out."

"I'm sorry to hear that. You're working here?" she asked with confusion as she looked around.

*Breathe. Breathe. Breathe.*

"Actually, I own it."

"Wow. That's wonderful. We heard amazing things about this place and had to come check it out for ourselves. Little did I know that my daughter owned it." She smiled.

"Hi, Anna, I'm Paul. It's finally nice to meet you," her husband spoke as he extended his hand.

"Hi, Paul. It's nice to meet you."

*I hated them. I wished they leave.*

"Wow, look at you. I can't believe I'm going to be a grandma."

*The fuck you are.*

I gave her a small fake smile.

"Are you married?" she asked.

*Like she couldn't tell from the rock on my finger. Oh, that's right, I wasn't wearing it because my fingers were so swollen.*

"Yes. I'm married to a wonderful man."

"I would love to talk to you, Anna. Is there any way we could do that?"

She was the last person I wanted to talk to. But all I could hear in my head was Dr. Stark's voice telling me that I needed closure with my mother and the only way to get that closure and be free from the hate and anger I harbored my entire life was to talk to her. I just didn't think the time would be now. If I rejected her, I'd only be screwing up my therapy. Plus, I was happy and in a better place now than I had been my whole life. I could handle her and a conversation. No problem.

"I guess so," I said.

"Why don't the two of you do it now?" Paul smiled. "Go grab some lunch. I'll head back to the hotel for a while."

"Is now okay with you?" she asked.

"I guess now is as good a time as any."

I wasn't sure a restaurant setting would be such a good place and it was a beautiful warm sunny day out, so I suggested we go talk in Central Park and grab a couple hot dogs. I couldn't help but stare at her. She looked a lot healthier than the last time I saw her. We had the same eyes and the same smile.

"What happened between you and your father?" she asked.

"You mean the father that never loved me? The father who sent me all the way across the country to boarding school so he didn't have to deal with me? The same father who disowned me and fired me from the family company because I didn't want to marry the man he thought I should?"

She slowly closed her eyes.

"Anna, I'm so sorry."

We took a seat on one of the benches in Central Park.

"You should be," I spoke in a harsh tone. "And now that you're here and we're talking after all these years, I want the answer to the question I had ever since I was five years old. Why? Why didn't you get the help you needed after I was born? How could you just abandon your child? Your flesh and blood? The person you carried inside you for nine months?"

"I can't answer that because I don't know. I did see a doctor once. Your father forced me to and he put me on medication, but the medication made me worse. My depression deepened and I felt like everything was hopeless. Your father grew angrier with me every day. You were constantly trying to get my attention and I was so absorbed in my own head and dark world that I was afraid of what I might do to you." She pulled up her sleeves and turned her wrists over where scars lay on her skin.

"I couldn't do it anymore. I felt like such a failure to you and your father and I didn't know how to help myself, so I tried to take my own life. Do you remember?"

I sat there, thinking as hard as I could.

"I was five years old and I remember Dad screaming at the nanny to get me out of the house and take me away until he called her. I never knew what happened that night. It was never talked about, and when the nanny brought me home, you were gone."

"Your father had me committed to a psychiatric hospital. While I was in there, he filed for divorce. I was granted supervised visitations, and I was ridden with guilt. That's why I didn't show some of the time. But when I finally worked up the courage to come see you and I looked into your eyes, I saw your hatred towards me. You knew I abandoned you and you weren't having any part of it. That's when I knew you'd grow up to be a strong independent woman with a strong will and mind. After that, I stayed away because I knew that was what was best for you. I don't blame you, Anna, for hating me. I hate myself too for what I'd done. After a few years and being on medication, I met Paul and he wanted children. I talked about you all the time and he was the one who convinced me to go see you in Connecticut. When I contacted your father to tell him I wanted to see you, he told me he sent you away. My heart broke and I needed to make sure you were okay. But, when I got there, you refused to see me."

"I couldn't see you. I hated you," I spoke.

"And rightfully so."

"The only reason I'm talking to you now is because my therapist told me that I needed closure with you."

"You're in therapy?" she asked.

"Not so much now, but I was, because I almost lost my husband."

"Why?"

"Because I told him I was never having children. That's what you and Dad did to me!"

"Anna," she softly spoke as tears filled her eyes.

"So I went to therapy for my lifelong issues and he helped me realize some things. He helped me realize that I'm not you and that I'll never be you."

"I want you to know that I never once stopping loving you or thinking about you. My two children know about you and they know what I did. I talk about you all the time."

All of a sudden, a severe cramping overtook me as I placed my hand on my belly and doubled over.

"Whoa!" I yelled.

"Anna, what's wrong?"

"Just a cramp."

"Have you been experiencing them all day?"

"Yes, but they're just Braxton Hicks. I think I just need to go home," I spoke as I got up from the bench.

We began walking towards the entrance of the park when another one hit me.

"Holy shit!" I yelled as my mother took hold of my arm.

"That was too close, Anna. I think you're in labor."

"I'm not in labor, Mother. I'm not due for another two and a half weeks."

"You were born at thirty-seven weeks. Babies come when they're ready. They don't care how many more weeks are left or have passed."

## CHAPTER THIRTY-EIGHT

*Wes*

My meeting finally ended, so I pulled out my phone on the way back to my office and noticed I had three missed calls from Anna and a voicemail. I brought my phone up to my ear to listen to her message.

"Wes, just so we're clear, I'm going to kill you when I see you for not answering your phone! I'm on my way to the hospital. I'm in labor. Get there as fast as you can."

"SHIT!" I yelled as I ran out of the building and hailed a cab.

The driver pulled up to the entrance of the ER and I threw some cash at him and told him to keep the change. Running through the doors, I saw Franco standing at the nurses' station.

"Franco, where is she?"

"I just got here myself. I'm trying to find out."

"Where is my wife? She came here in labor. Her name is Anna Carter."

"Your wife has been taken up to the OB unit, Mr. Carter. Take the elevators up to the fifth floor and the nurses will take you to her."

"Thank you. Come on, Franco."

We took the elevators up, and when we stepped off, I rang the buzzer on the door.

"May I help you?" a female voice spoke.

"My wife is up here in labor. Her name is Anna Carter."

The door buzzed and Franco and I went inside.

"Mr. Carter, I'm Casey, your wife's nurse. Follow me and I'll take you to her."

We followed the nurse down the hall and into Anna's room. The moment I saw her, I ran to her bedside.

"Sweetheart." I kissed her forehead. "I'm so sorry. I was in a meeting."

"I figured." She squeezed my hand.

"How are you, Momma?" Franco smiled as he grabbed her other hand.

"I'm okay. But once a contraction hits, you might want to run."

"Wes, there's something—"

"Anna, I brought you some ice chips," a woman walked into the room.

"Holy Mary mother of God," Franco spoke as he stared at her. "That's Anna's mother."

"What?" I looked at Anna.

"It's a long story."

"Franco, isn't it?" She smiled. "Look at you. You've grown up into a handsome man."

"Hello, Anna's mother. Long time no see."

"I didn't know you and Anna were still friends," she said.

"Anna and I will be best friends until the day we die."

"You must be Anna's husband." She extended her hand to me.

"Yes, I'm Wes Carter." I lightly shook her hand. "May I ask why you're here?"

"I was wondering the same thing," Franco spoke.

"My husband Paul and I were in the cupcake shop. I had no idea that Anna owned the place. We went to talk in Central Park, and she went into labor."

"Are you living in New York?" Franco asked.

"No. Not yet anyway. We're here looking at places to live."

"Oh," Franco said as he looked over at Anna.

I looked at Franco and tilted my head towards the door, gesturing that he take Anna's mother out of the room so the two of us could talk.

"Anna's mom, why don't you come with me and we'll go get a nice cup of coffee. Tell me what you've been up all these years." He smiled as he placed his hand on her arm.

"Sure. Okay. And please, call me Carla."

They left the room and I looked at Anna, leaned in, and kissed her lips.

"Are you all right? Is she the reason you went into labor? Did you get yourself all worked up?"

"No, Wes. She's not the reason. I guess those weren't Braxton Hicks I was having all morning. And, I'm fine. We talked. When I went into labor, she had a security guard get me a wheelchair and she wheeled me out of the park and got us a cab. She was yelling at the driver to step on it. For the first time in my life, she took care of me."

"That's good, sweetheart." I pressed my lips against her forehead. I still had my concerns.

After eight hours of labor, our daughter, Aubrey Paris Carter, was born at six pounds, ten ounces. She was beautiful and looked exactly like Anna. I was going to have my hands full with her and the boys. I could already tell.

I sat by Anna's bedside as she breastfed her for the first time. I had a family. A beautiful family who were my entire reason for breathing. I stepped out of the room and called Dr. Stark to tell him the news and to also tell him that Anna's mother was in town.

"Dr. Stark," he answered.

"Dr. Stark, it's Wes Carter."

"Wes, how are you?"

"I'm good. Anna had the baby."

"Excellent. How is she doing?"

"She's good, but there's another reason I called. Her mother is here with us. They went to Central Park to talk and Anna went into labor."

"Hmm. Okay. I'll come by the hospital and pay Anna a visit, in case she wants to talk about it."

"Thanks, Dr. Stark. I appreciate it."

## CHAPTER THIRTY-NINE
### Three Months Later

*Anna*

The love I felt for my daughter was so overwhelming, I didn't think it was possible. I sat on the bed with my back against the headboard and my baby on my legs. She was alert and awake as I talked to her and told her how much I loved her.

"There are my two favorite girls in the whole world." Wes smiled as he walked into the room and kissed us both.

"How was your day?" I asked.

"It was all right. I spent most of it missing the two of you."

"Is that why you're home so early?" I smirked.

"Actually, it is." He smiled as he picked up Aubrey. "If you need to rest, then rest. My daughter and I are going to spend some time together."

"I pumped some bottles today. Don't forget, it's your turn to get up with her tonight."

"I haven't forgotten, sweetheart. We'll be downstairs if you want to join us." He kissed my head.

Wes was the perfect father. In fact, he was too perfect, and I feared little Miss Aubrey was going to be incredibly spoiled by him. But not only by her daddy, but also by her uncle and godfather, Franco.

After Aubrey was born, I continued my therapy sessions with Dr. Stark, and I continued my yoga and meditation. Everything I feared all these years about having children was for nothing. Now I couldn't imagine my life without her.

My mother and I slowly started to get to know each other. She was a different person now than when she had me and I realized that everyone deserved a second chance. She was good with Aubrey and I could tell she loved her. I had finally met my half-siblings. I had a sister and a brother. Allie was twenty-one and Michael was nineteen. Wes was afraid that all of this was too soon and that I'd be overwhelmed, but I wasn't. All of a sudden, I had this instant family and I embraced it.

When I think back to the chain of events that led me to Wes, I knew he was the one I was meant to be with for the rest of my life. The natural forces of the world made sure we met in Paris, and they also made sure it didn't end there. One night in Paris was all it took to change my life forever.

"Anna, can you take her please?" Wes asked as he walked into the room and handed her to me. "She's been changed and now I need to do the same."

I looked at his shirt and couldn't help but laugh.

"Did she?" I asked.

"Yes. How does one child have that much poop in her? She exploded all over me."

He took off his clothes and went into the bathroom to clean up. Once he changed, he climbed on the bed next to us, hooked his arm around me, and placed his finger in his daughter's hand while she wrapped her tiny fingers around it.

"I love us." He smiled as he looked at me.

"I love us too." I kissed his lips.

"When can we start working on the next one?"

"When can you stop asking such silly questions?"

"Right." He grinned as he kissed me.

# BOOKS BY SANDI LYNN

If you haven't already done so, please check out my other books. Escape from reality and into the world of romance. I'll take you on a journey of love, pain, heartache and happily ever afters.

**Millionaires:**

The Forever Series (Forever Black, Forever You, Forever Us, Being Julia, Collin, A Forever Christmas, A Forever Family)

Love, Lust & A Millionaire (Wyatt Brothers, Book 1)

Love, Lust & Liam (Wyatt Brothers, Book 2)

Lie Next To Me (A Millionaire's Love, Book 1)

When I Lie with You (A Millionaire's Love, Book 2)

Then You Happened (Happened Series, Book 1)

Then We Happened (Happened Series, Book 2)

His Proposed Deal

A Love Called Simon

The Seduction of Alex Parker

Something About Lorelei

One Night In London

The Exception

Corporate A$$

A Beautiful Sight

The Negotiation

Defense

Playing The Millionaire

#Delete

Behind His Lies

Carter Grayson (Redemption Series, Book One)

Chase Calloway (Redemption Series, Book Two)

Jamieson Finn (Redemption Series, Book Three)

The Interview: New York & Los Angeles Part 1

The Interview: New York & Los Angeles Part 2

Rewind

**Second Chance Love:**

Remembering You

She Writes Love

Love In Between (Love Series, Book 1)

The Upside of Love (Love Series, Book 2)

**Sports:**

Lightning

# ABOUT THE AUTHOR

Sandi Lynn is a New York Times, USA Today and Wall Street Journal bestselling author who spends all her days writing. She published her first novel, *Forever Black*, in February 2013 and hasn't stopped writing since. Her addictions are shopping, going to the gym, romance novels, coffee, chocolate, margaritas, and giving readers an escape to another world.

**Be a part of my tribe and make sure to sign up for my newsletter so you don't miss a Sandi Lynn book again!**

**Facebook:** www.facebook.com/Sandi.Lynn.Author
  **Twitter:** www.twitter.com/SandilynnWriter
  **Website:** www.authorsandilynn.com
  **Pinterest:** www.pinterest.com/sandilynnWriter
  **Instagram:** www.instagram.com/sandilynnauthor
  **Goodreads:** http://bit.ly/2w6tN25
  **Newsletter:** http://bit.ly/2Rzoz2L

Printed in Poland
by Amazon Fulfillment
Poland Sp. z o.o., Wrocław